Resounding praise for the novels of
VALERIE WILSON WESLEY

"A welcome voice and a fresh point of view."
USA Today

"Valerie Wilson Wesley has tapped into
the strengths and frailties of men, women,
family friends—and marriage."
Sandra Kitt, author of *Family Affairs*

"There's a richness of language in Wesley's writing,
joined by a delightful sense of humor."
San Francisco Examiner

"It isn't necessary to be black to understand
and enjoy the prolific Ms. Wesley. . . .
[She] speaks to universals."
Dallas Morning News

"[Her] characters are believable
and Wesley has a keen ear for dialogue."
Washington Post Book World

"Valerie Wilson Wesley tells a funny, wise tale . . .
and she tells it very well."
Bebe Moore Campbell, author of *Singin' in the Comeback Choir*

By Valerie Wilson Wesley

Playing My Mother's Blues
Always True to You in My Fashion
Ain't Nobody's Business If I Do

The Tamara Hayle Mysteries

When Death Comes Stealing
Devil's Gonna Get Him
Where Evil Sleeps
No Hiding Place
Easier to Kill
The Devil Riding
Dying in the Dark

Books for Children

Willimena Rules!
   How to Lose Your Class Pet
   How to Fish for Trouble
   How to Lose Your Cookie Money
   How to (Almost) Ruin Your School Play
Freedom's Gift: A Juneteenth Story

PLAYING MY MOTHER'S BLUES

VALERIE WILSON WESLEY

AVON BOOKS
An Imprint of HarperCollinsPublishers

This book was originally published in hardcover by William Morrow in March 2005 and in trade paperback by Avon Books in June 2006.

AVON BOOKS
An Imprint of HarperCollins*Publishers*
10 East 53rd Street
New York, New York 10022-5299

Copyright © 2005 by Valerie Wilson Wesley
ISBN: 978-0-06-101553-3
ISBN-10: 0-06-101553-9
www.avonromance.com

First Avon Books mass market paperback printing: February 2007
First Avon Books trade paperback printing: June 2006
First William Morrow hardcover printing: March 2005

Avon Trademark Reg. U.S. Pat. Off. and in Other Countries, Marca Registrada, Hecho en U.S.A.
HarperCollins® is a registered trademark of HarperCollins Publishers.

Printed in the U.S.A.

10 9 8 7 6 5 4 3 2 1

For Pat

Friday

Mariah

one

I talk to ghosts these days; they are my only company. We speak at odd and sundry moments—when the morning sun peeks into my bedroom, while I'm sitting on the bus to work, as I sip one of the two mixed drinks I allow myself before dinner. Events that occurred decades ago haunt me. My life is filled with phantoms.

The most persistent, of course, is the man whose life I took. Mine was a crime of rage and passion. He shows up at night before I fall asleep. Even after all these years, I can feel him enter my bed, touch my foot with his, pull me toward him against my will.

My daughters, Dani and Rose, who are both still alive and always a pleasure to see, arrive with first light. I see them as I saw them last, Dani as a little girl, Rose near womanhood. I talk to Dani as if she were still my baby, trying on my crazy earrings, dancing in my shoes, spraying herself with my cologne. Rose looks as she did on the night that changed us both, but I try to forget that image and replace it with one of her laughing as she used to when she would tease or scold me.

My ex-husband, Hilton Dells, appears when I least expect him. He'll show up suddenly, some small incident calling him up. Like today on my job, when Irish, the cashier who works the station next to me, was carrying on about this wedding she saw on TV.

"Did you see it?" she asked, and the girls at the other stations all began talking at once, giving lengthy descriptions of the dress the bride wore, the flowers in her bouquet, the engagement ring on her finger. That was when I thought of Hilton Dells and my own wedding, which none of the chattering women could have imagined.

My wedding dress was made in Paris. His choice, not mine; I was too foolish to be insulted by his presumption. I wore his mother's diamond ring. He once told me it was the only thing of value she had ever owned. I should have kept it; it would be of value to me right about now. I left it on my pillow the night I left them. I gave back everything he'd given me—dresses, jewelry, furs, everything except the two things I valued most, which he snatched away.

I've never liked weddings.

"Well, did you see it?" Irish was impatient for my answer. Her real name is Bernadette but we call her Irish, because even though she's been here fifteen years, she still has an Irish accent that gives a charming lilt to everything she says. "Did you see it when he gave her that last kiss? So what did you think?"

"Pretty cool," I said.

"Pretty cool! Maria, is that all you can say?"

I'm known here as Maria, the name my mother gave me. I was a number at Somerset—1054836. When I got out, I realized "Mariah," the name I once called myself, belonged to the past; Mariah died with Durrell Alexander.

I chuckled at Irish's excitement about the TV wedding, which brought another question.

"Maria, where *is* your mind?" Irish has reddish-brown hair that she tucks under a cap, and eyes so green they look fake. She's pretty but carries too much weight for someone her age.

It was going on eleven, and the Friday-morning shoppers had come and gone; the ones who shop at lunchtime hadn't yet arrived.

"Maria?"

"Yeah, it was good, wasn't it?" I said, my mind returning from another of its journeys. Irish is thirty and married, with two kids and a disabled husband whom she adores. She goes to school at night to "better" herself. I liked her the moment I laid eyes on her because she's the same age my Dani is now.

But she's not Dani. She's "Irish," with curls that slip out of her cap, an angelic grin, and a bigoted husband who hates black people. She probably assumes I'm Hispanic because of my coloring and my name; most of the women at Somerset did even though I constantly told them what I was. By the time I left, I spoke Spanish with the best of them; it was easier that way.

"Maria, have you ever been married?"

"Yeah. Long time ago." I should have lied; I usually do. But it's hard to lie to a woman who reminds you so much of your daughter.

"Divorced?"

"Yep."

"I wish my wedding had been like that one on TV, with a long dress and a lacy veil and a big diamond ring I could wear instead of this old thing." She held out her hands. I noticed that she'd bitten her nails to the quick the way I used to.

"What was your wedding like, Maria?"

"Justice of the peace. Fast and easy. The ceremony, not the marriage. That lasted longer than it should have." That is the most I've told anyone about the life I led before I moved back here and began working in the store.

"Wanna get some lunch? Grab something at Dean's? They got specials on Friday."

"Not today, honey. I brought my own. Next week? I'll treat."

"Really?" Her eyes lit up.

Sure. That's me. Big-time spender, Maria.

Irish gave me a sunny grin, and I realized how fond I've become of her.

But not too fond. I keep to myself as much as I can. I don't like to explain to people who I was before and where I spent the last twenty years of my life. I treasure my solitude. I'm addicted to silence and privacy; I wallow in it. A sandwich eaten alone in some quiet clean place is a pleasure I never deny myself.

When we broke for lunch, I took the tuna on a roll I'd wrapped in foil out of my cubby inside the employees' room and sat down at the desk by the window. It rained hard last night, but this morning made up for it. The sun shone brightly, and I moved close to the window, enjoying the feel of it on my forehead. There were days in Somerset when I couldn't catch a glimpse of it, and certainly I never felt it with only glass between us. I closed my eyes to savor its warmth.

After a while, I went to the vending machine for a bag of Fritos and a Coke, then came back to my spot at the window and gazed out at the sky as I munched my sandwich. I never tire of watching the clouds make shapes. It makes me remember a game I used to play with Dani, imagining animals in the sky, seeing them come and wondering where they would go. Somebody had forgotten a newspaper on the bench next to the desk, and I picked it up and thumbed through it as I sipped the last of my Coke. The article on Hilton Dells's death took up half the page.

He'd died on Wednesday morning after a short illness, it said. I felt nothing as I read it; even seeing his photograph had no effect. Hilton had always been vain, and the photo was that of a man in his fifties; he must have been eighty if a day. I ripped it out and stuffed it in my pocket.

Later that night when I was at home, I pulled out the article and read it as I sipped the first of my drinks. When I finished it, I folded it into a small, tight square and sank back on my couch.

I live in a small furnished apartment in a six-story building only a few miles from the grand house where I once lived with my daughters. They are on different sides of the world. My living room is a pukey shade of yellow, and the upholstery of the couch, which is old and squeaks when I sit down, picks up the color. There is a small red Formica table in the galley kitchen with two chairs, one of which needs mending. My bedroom is the same shade of yellow as the living room, but the morning sun comes in full and makes it bright. My bed is comfortable; I'm grateful for that.

Even though the furnishings are not what I would choose, the place is clean without vermin, which is a relief. It's better than the cell I left three years ago and the rooms I've lived in since. I find comfort and safety in small spaces, so I'm comfortable here. I recently bought an old chest at a rummage sale that serves as my coffee table. It's a good one, mahogany; the seller had no idea how valuable it was. That was one thing I learned from Hilton Dells, to know good furniture when I saw it. This chest and television are the only things here that belong to me.

I took a hearty swallow of my drink, vodka and tonic tonight, closed my eyes, and waited for the calm it brings.

His memorial service would be held tomorrow afternoon at two. It would take place in that building of which he was always so proud. I remembered every inch of that damned place, the biggest, grandest, costliest ever owned by a black man in the city, he would boast.

"Well, old bastard, I beat you after all!" I said.

On generous days, I admit to myself that I blame him more than I should. He did the only thing he could do considering what happened between us. We were mismatched from the first. But it wasn't only years that separated us, although those prone to sympathize with me assumed that was the problem. Twenty years between a man and woman is a long time, even though Hilton never looked his age. He was good-looking at forty, and probably was on the day he died. He wasn't a cruel man either, not at first anyway. I'm not sure how much I changed him, probably as much as he did me. A marriage is a living thing, and when it's as poisonous as ours was, so deadly at its roots, it kills everything that springs from it.

But I wasn't a child when I left him for Durrell. I was thirty-seven years old, a grown woman by anyone's standards, old enough to know what I was doing. I had just begun to notice those subtle signs of aging—the tiny pouches under my eyes when I woke in the morning, the slight flabbiness around my belly, the subtle droop of my breasts. Hilton was aging, too, in more obvious ways. I didn't want to grow old with him.

My mother introduced us. At first I thought she wanted him for herself.

"Hilton, this is my daughter Maria," she said in the sparkling voice she pulled out when talking to attractive men.

"I'm so glad to finally meet you," I said with a charming smile, my eyes wide and innocent. I

"Hilton has been helping me with your grand-mother's estate." She explained in one sentence that he was a man who knew and respected money. I didn't learn until later just how much he knew about money and how much it obsessed him. Later that week, he took us both to lunch and then me to dinner. From the start, he knew what he wanted, and for reasons I didn't under-stand, he wanted me.

At twenty, I believed myself a miserable pack-age. My life was stuck in place, going nowhere. The money my grandmother left us kept me from needing to find work right away, but my mother and I knew that wouldn't last forever. I'd planned to enroll in Gibbs Secretarial School, a college near where we lived, in the fall, with the idea (planted by mother) that I might land a job with a rich boss whom I could charm. I had no ambition of my own.

It was 1962, the year Kennedy sent the feds to Mississippi, and black and white kids who boarded Greyhounds to intergrate the South were chased back home by bloodhounds. Rosa Parks had ridden that bus, Dr. King had raised some Cain, and folks were going to jail for sitting at lunch counters at Woolworth's and Kresge's. I stopped shopping in those stores for my makeup and fabric, but I didn't identify with being black. I wasn't sure what I was or how I was supposed to feel. My mother didn't help the situation. Whenever she could, she passed for white.

"You simply don't correct them," she explained, surprised that I would care.

"But it's lying. You're not white, and neither am I!"

"You are what you look like, and most people in the North are too polite to ask. This isn't the South. They make assumptions based upon your color and your hair, so you simply keep your mouth shut. We look as white as most of them, if you don't look too close. It's their mistake, not yours."

Her attitude, of course, left us with no meaningful ties to the black community. We had no connections to anyone, black or white, except to a few Swedish immigrants left over from her childhood and several color-struck women whose paths had crossed ours at various points in our lives. We had no tribe; we were on our own. Until she saw "the light" in the person of a handsome forty-year-old man looking for a woman who would be willing to do what he said.

Hilton had no time for wooing or winning a woman's heart; acquiring a wife was similar to purchasing property. She should have certain attributes—and beauty was certainly one of them. She had to be reasonably intelligent—no dull heirs for him. Mostly, he wanted someone he could mold, in the manner of some nineteenth-century patriarch. So I jumped from the arms of a domineering, omniscient mother into those of a similar husband. I didn't mind at first.

There was the money, which didn't take long to get used to. Hilton liked to see me dressed well, since I was a reflection of him, and he took great pains to teach me what to wear, where to shop, what was stylish. His taste was good, so shopping in those first few years was a grand adventure. He genuinely enjoyed it, as if fulfilling some feminine, neglected part of himself.

When I met Lucille, his bitch of a sister, I saw his neglected part in the flesh. We were the same age, yet mixed like oil and water. Maybe she sensed something about me. She had her brother's keen instincts about people. She took me in, swirled me around, and spat me out like mouthwash.

Lucille Dells is one ghost from my past I hope never pays me a visit.

Hilton made her the godmother for our daughters even though I wanted to ask my friend Trish, the only friend I'd kept from high school. Trish died of a brain tumor the year before I got out of Somerset. She is a ghost who has never come to visit but was always good company when she was alive. I would welcome her presence.

Rose was born the year after I was married. I'd

just turned twenty-one. She was a pretty baby, with hair so lovely other mothers would stop me on the street just to touch it. I took delight in that. As I was an extension of Hilton, Rose was one of me, and I was the perfect, doting mother. My daughter reflected me, and I loved her because of that.

This is what I tell my daughters when they make their morning calls: I ask Dani to forgive me for leaving her so soon. I beg Rose for her forgiveness, for me not knowing and acknowledging who she was until it was too late, for the sorrow I brought down on both of us. I pray I've left them some good.

Mothers need to believe they've taught their daughters more than they actually have. That was my mother's mistake.

"Now I can die knowing you will be safe," she told me shortly after Rose was born. It was morning, and I was nursing. The baby's suckling made me feel relaxed and sensual; it was far more enjoyable than I'd imagined it could be.

"Why would you say something like that?" I glanced up, my face dull with pleasure.

"You're enjoying that too much!"

"How can you enjoy nursing your own baby too much?"

"Don't raise your voice, you'll sour your milk!"

"How can raising my voice sour my milk?" I said, laughing at her.

"Listen to what I say, I know far more than you."

"Yes, Mother!" I said, and laughed. Since my baby's birth, a new ease had developed between us. We spoke more as friends than mother and daughter. I saw her great weakness: she believed in Hilton Dells more than in me or herself.

"I won't live to see the end of summer." I shook my head in mock disgust. She was always dramatic, and it wasn't the first time she'd spoken of death. That was May. She was dead by September.

Maybe she'd been sick for months and simply never told me. Could that have been why she urged me to marry a man she knew I didn't love?

"Why?" I ask her now when she visits. "What was in it for you?"

"Comfort," she tells me in her matter-of-fact voice. "And anyway, I didn't force you. I didn't have a choice."

"But didn't you know what kind of man he was? What would happen to me in twenty years?"

"I'm dead now. Leave me alone," she'll say from that part of myself where she still lives, and I let her rest in peace.

But I missed her after she died. I still do. I depended on her, and when she left, there was no one. Except for Trish, all of my friends were his, and he had grown distant and moody. He doled out love in portions: a dollop of sympathy after my mother died; small change to run the household; joyless, stingy sex. On Friday nights, he expected it with no spontaneity or intimacy. I was a virgin when we married, so I had no idea what else it could be; that must have been one of his prerequisites. His dullness pulled me in, and I became part of it.

So for ten years we played our roles, attending the parties and dinners that came with his status. He placed his arm around my shoulders, smoothing my fur, opening my doors, bringing me drinks from the bars. Nothing was real for me. Not in all that time.

I was thirty when Dani was born, the same age she is now. I hope that she is happier than I was then. If I was obsessed with Rose, I neglected Dani. She was an independent little soul, a happy child who cried very little, but I was always distracted, my body restless.

"You are overwhelmed by motherhood," Trish would tell me when she'd come to visit, which was often in the spring of 1978. Dani was in school by then, and Rose was a teenager. Trish and I were still close, although I'd never shared the emptiness in my marriage; I didn't realize how empty it had become.

"I love being a mother." I was defensive, well aware of the different paths we'd taken. Trish, always smart and ambitious, had gone right from high school to college and then straight to graduate school in journalism. She worked for a black women's magazine, and I envied her. I don't think she envied me.

"Motherhood is fine, but there's somebody underneath all that selflessness. There's my old friend Maria, or have you forgotten her?"

It was a Thursday afternoon late in March when we had that conversation. I could smell spring, even though there was still snow on the ground. It made me feel optimistic and daring. That morning I'd given our caretaker, a Jamaican man with strong hands and beautiful eyes, instructions on where I wanted things planted, and noticed for the first time how good-looking he was.

"Look at yourself!" Trish pulled me in front of my bedroom mirror. I looked at my image and felt older than thirty-six. My skin was dry and my hair, pulled back in a knot, made me into a stereotype of an aging spinster. Trish pulled the elastic out of my hair. I shook my head, and it swung loose around my face.

"I look like a wild woman."

"You've got to let that wild woman come out."

"But I'll have to shove her back before Hilton gets home."

"The hell with Hilton! You've got to cut this mess off." She ran her fingers through my long hair. "Most people cut their hair in the sixties.

You're almost too late. You should wear it natural. Cut it short, in your own style. Whatever it looked like, it would look better than it looks now."

"I like my hair," I said, pulling it back up.

"Maybe you like it too much, have you ever thought about that? It's past time you embraced the *African* in you."

I laughed when she said that because Trish's politics were far more radical than mine. She'd been involved in the civil rights movement from the beginning, and now her interest had spread to the women's movement and politics. She had applied to law school, and was constantly angry about everything—from environmental racism to the Supreme Court decision in the *Bakke* case. "It's time you got rid of it. Cut off those European roots you're so proud of."

"You know me better than that!" I said, well aware that I was one of the few unenlightened women my radical friend still spoke to.

We stood together in the mirror, me with my hair in an untidy bun, Trish with her short, smart natural that emphasized her sharp cheekbones and beautiful skin. Her gold earrings in the shape of wolves, a Native American symbol of empowerment, she told me, caught the sun and glittered. My mother used to say it was bad luck for two people to share the same mirror. I know now she was right.

"And while we're talking about it, look at these hands! When was the last time those nails saw a coat of polish?"

I glanced down at my fingernails, which were bitten to the quick.

"On me." She grabbed my poor, neglected fingers. "I have a gift certificate from this spa over on Eighty-sixth Street, and you can get a manicure and a pedicure on me. I'll even pay for a new haircut. Early birthday present. Tomorrow morning, first thing."

"Not too new!"

"You're hiding in your hair. You need a new you! It will grow back if you miss it too much. Don't worry!"

So we went to the spa that Friday, and Trish threw in a facial as well. When I came out that afternoon, my hair was so short I could feel the spring breeze fanning my scalp on its way to my ears. It tickled my head and made me laugh out loud.

"He's not going to like it." I pulled my manicured fingers through my hair, touching my scalp, thrilled by the feel of it. I hadn't realized how sensuous the touch of fingers, even my own, could be. It was a new sense of nakedness, and I felt free and lighthearted.

"Looks good, sis!" Trish lightly touched my hair, then gave me a hug. "So you are coming to

my party Saturday night for your coming out?" It
was an order rather than a question.

"I'll have to let you know. I've got to find a sit-
ter, I've—"

"*He's* there. Just come. Tell him we're having
dinner together, then leave."

"I don't like to lie to him."

"There will be dinner, of a sort!"

"Let me think about it."

"Be there!"

That made me laugh, the way she said it. But
my mood darkened when I thought about facing
Hilton.

"Mommy, what happened to your hair?" Dani
screamed when I walked into the house later that
day. She giggled as she ran her fingers over my
head. "I can feel your scalp!"

"Nice feeling, huh?"

She tugged on her braids. "Can I cut mine, too?"

"Sure, maybe this summer when it gets hot."

"Hey, Ma, you look hip!" Rose glanced over her
book and chimed in her opinion. "Now your hair
matches those weird earrings you're always buying!" Rose teased me relentlessly about my taste
in earrings. I loved oversized hoops in copper or
gold, because they reminded me of gypsies. They
were my only concession to contemporary fash-
ions. I wore the diamonds my husband gave me
when we went out at night.

Hilton said nothing. No comment. No criticism. No disapproval. It was our "sex" night, but he didn't touch me.

That was probably the reason I showed up at Trish's apartment on Saturday for my night of "firsts": first time leaving home without telling a damn soul where I was going; first time getting drunk and smoking pot; first time seeing Durrell Alexander.

And until the moment I shot him, I couldn't take my eyes away.

two

$\mathcal{I}$t was an old story, me and Durrell Alexander. As old as dumb, restless women and cruel-hearted men.

"So who are you?" His first words to me.

"Maria."

"Mariah?"

Maybe the marijuana I'd smoked with Trish earlier slurred my speech or the stereo played so loudly he couldn't hear me good, but when he said that name, Mariah, easing down toward me like he did, his breath grazing my ear, it was so musical I didn't correct him. I simply nodded that he was right.

"You a friend of Trish?"

I nodded again, afraid to trust my voice. His was deep with a playful lilt, as if he might burst out laughing or tease you for no good reason. I couldn't place the accent. It had a British cadence, as if he were from the West Indies, but I knew Jamaican accents, and it wasn't that. I found out later it was Charleston by way of Memphis trying to be something else. It took him awhile to tell me that and other things about himself, like where he came from and what his life had been until he showed up in New York City.

He was the youngest son of an illiterate teenage mother and an older man as charming as he was violent and absent. His teenage years were spent with an aunt in Memphis bent on making him pay for her sister's early sins. She dragged him to Pentecostal churches where he prayed for salvation, asked for forgiveness, and talked in tongues, but at night he escaped to blues clubs, bars, and old movie theaters where he watched old movies and slept until dawn.

He spent two years in a small Southern college, where he discovered poetry and his keen eye for photography. Those were the early years of popular black movies—*Shaft, Lady Sings the Blues, Black Caesar*—and film with its magical promise of instant success and escape drew him in. He was a quick learner and fast talker, so when he made his way to Manhattan his wit and talent made him the center of attention long before his independent film. But there was a hole within him, a wound left from his early years that was deeper

even than my own. I had to fall in before I could
see it.

There was no hint of it that night. He was strik-
ing, tall and elegant, the first man I saw when I
walked into the place. His lanky, graceful body
swayed rhythmically to the music as if it belonged to the sound and he was unaware of its
movement. People were dressed in all manner of
things: t-shirts and jeans, jogging suits and silk.
Dresses of every conceivable length, dropping
from the top of panties down to the floor. Plat-
form shoes shuffled with sandals. Studded
denim, embroidered suede, Halston and Stephen
Burrows. Disco touched with "pimp" in rainbow
colors. But he was dressed in black like some
stranded pirate. He was, of course, surrounded by
women.

High from grass, I'd trotted behind Trish like a
lost puppy. She settled me into an easy chair and
dashed off to the kitchen to look after her famous
chili. I felt awkward and dizzy, so I closed my eyes.

"So, Mariah. You got a last name?" Until he
spoke, I hadn't noticed he'd settled next to me on
the couch.

"Dells."

"Mariah Dells. Nice name. Good ring to it. I
like it," he said, as if his liking my name was sig-
nificant and I should be pleased, and I grinned
back, strangely at ease. His smile always did that

to me. That was one of the good things about him, the way he made me feel. In the beginning, anyway.

"What's your name?" I found my voice.

"Durrell. Durrell Alexander. I make films." He volunteered it with a self-assured cockiness that meant I should recognize it. After he was dead, I found out that name was a lie. His name was Darnell. Darnell Anderson. At least the initials were the same.

"So you're famous?" My naïveté peeked through. He gave me a strange look, as if I were being sarcastic, then grinned good-naturedly.

"Depends who you ask." We both laughed then, me because I was high and everything sounded funny, and him because it was true. "Let me get you a drink. Wine, brew, what you want?"

"Wine is good."

"You look like a red wine woman."

"No, pink. Rosé."

He laughed as if I had said something funny. "You're the first woman I've met since I've been in this goddam city who actually admits to drinking rosé wine. Mateus, I'll bet."

"What's wrong with rosé?" I didn't know much about wine, I just liked the name. I didn't tell him that.

"Not a damn thing, if Trish has got some. I wouldn't count on it, though. She's a red wine type. Rioja. Beaujolais. Or scotch on the rocks if that's the kind of place she's at."

I wasn't sure what he meant by that. "I'll try red, then."

"Got something else you'll like, too." He nodded toward Trish's bedroom, where they were smoking pot.

"I'm high already, thank you, and I've got to drive home."

"This will mellow you out. You'll be able to drive, play, whatever the hell you want to do, better than you did it before." He pulled out a cube of hashish and led me into the room, and after some wine and a few tokes of hash, I found out he was right. I felt like I could do whatever the hell I wanted. What I liked most, though, was the feel of his thigh against mine in that smoky room, the way he kept touching me, brushing my arms, my fingers, my breast. I liked the way he sucked on the hash pipe passionately, as if he were gasping for air, drawing in his last breath.

"You married, right?" he asked me later when he walked me to my car. It was hard to ignore Hilton's mother's ring sprouting like a growth on my left hand and harder still my black Lincoln, courtesy of Hilton, moored like a yacht among the Volkswagen Beetles and Fiats three blocks from Trish's place.

"Fancy car, rich married lady. I don't know if I can handle that. What you say about that?" He said it as if what would happen between us was a foregone conclusion, and when he kissed me, his tongue forcing its way between my lips, finding my tongue and sucking it, I knew that it was.

"I'll be in touch. Mariah, right?" His lips brushed my ear.

"Maria."

"I like Mariah better."

I could still taste him on my lips when I crawled into bed beside Hilton that night. I didn't sleep until dawn, his kiss had rooted itself so deep inside me.

I asked Trish about him later. I was glad when she told me he'd badgered her for my number and any other information he could get.

"I'm not going to cheat on my husband, he's just attractive," I told her.

"This is not a good idea, Maria." She'd been around long enough to know what I might get into, and she didn't like it.

"Mariah."

"What?"

"I've been thinking of changing my name, and that's what I've decided it will be."

"Why the hell are you doing that?"

"I'm just adding an *H*, that's all."

"That's what he called you, isn't it? Bastard!"

"That's what I'm calling myself. And why do you call him that?"

She didn't say anything after that, which was rare for Trish because she didn't like silences in conversation.

"So who is he?"

She hesitated, then told me what I wanted to know.

Durrell Alexander was a filmmaker, she said. His films were independent, not for popular consumption like the others aimed toward black folks that were pouring out of Hollywood. They were "serious" films, artistic. His first one was about a boy growing up in a brutal home with a nasty father, a failed musician who comes to a small Tennessee town from Harlem and ends up dead. When she said the name, I realized I'd actually heard of it. It had gotten good reviews and a lot of attention. Durrell told me later the film was based on his father, who died when he was fifteen, after he'd moved to Memphis. The second one, which had been out for about a year, hadn't done as well. He was still living off the money from the first, and it was running out. He desperately needed another hit, but nothing had come his way.

"Don't trust him," Trish said.

I figured her warning was sour grapes. He'd told me on the way to my car that Trish had been trying to get next to him ever since he met her, which was why he'd been invited to her party in the first place. I never asked her about it. Maybe she did have a thing for him, or maybe he was lying like he did about so many other things.

What I did know about him was that he had no respect for boundaries, but neither did I. My marriage to Hilton meant nothing to him because it meant nothing to me. Lying came easy to me then, and from the first night I met Durrell, he became the reason for my life. He defined me because I had no definition of myself. Hilton had given me his, and when I shook that off, I had nothing left.

Did you ever love me?

I ask Durrell that now when I speak to him at night.

I don't think he knew. He had told me once that he envied wealthy people, so maybe he saw Hilton Dells in me like so many others did. Maybe by possessing me, he possessed some part of what this rich black man stood for, and when *I* emerged, he couldn't stand it.

Why do you love me?

When I asked him the first time, he told me what I wanted to hear. He loved the way I looked, he said, that my skin was smooth like rich white folks' satin, my hair as soft as corn silk. He would say that when he washed it, played with it, his fingers touching my scalp as gently as Dani did that night I cut it off. In the beginning, he did that often. When I bathed, he would soap my hair in the tub, the smell of coconut shampoo filling that narrow hot room. He'd undress, climb in behind me, his legs easing next to mine in the slippery tub. He'd caress my hair, breasts, between my legs until I turned so he could slide inside me.

Tell me why you love me?

He'd answer with his fingers, lips, tongue.

I remember the first time we made love; grief and time have not erased that.

He lived on Central Park North, the top floor of a broken-down building off 110th Street on what they called a "good street" in Harlem, across from Central Park and within walking distance of Columbia. It was a sixth-floor walk-up, one bedroom, surprisingly spacious, with long windows that looked out at the park across the street and hardwood floors in need of a good polish. I drove over the George Washington Bridge that first time, and parked on a corner off of his street. We decided on noon; there was no traffic.

The place was sparsely furnished: a bed covered with a madras-print bedspread served as a couch, a black bentwood rocker was pushed into a corner, bookshelves made of planks and bricks that were crammed with paperbacks flanked three walls. He'd rescued a scratched maple bureau from the street, and polished it until it shone. The drawers, which had brass handles shaped like lions, were where he kept important things: copies of his films, extra money, a charm that belonged to his mother, an old revolver that he later told me belonged to his father. A wobbly card table that held an ancient Royal electric typewriter was pushed against a wall.

His bedroom was narrow, with only enough room for the bed and a cheap black sheepskin rug. A white chenille bedspread that belonged to his aunt was spread on the bed, an oddly feminine touch in an austere, masculine room. Wooden wind chimes hung in the window off of the fire escape, and when the breeze hit them they gave an Eastern sound to the place, as if we'd entered a room in some lush, exotic city.

He unbuttoned my blouse slowly; it was a silk one in forest green that I'd bought at Saks the day before because he'd mentioned that was his favorite color. He unhooked my lacy bra in a single motion, pulled down my half slip, stockings, black satin panties. His fingers caressed between my legs, then entered me hard. I shivered, excited to have part of him inside me. He kissed my throat, the space beneath my breasts, nipples, between my legs.

The bed smelled like myrrh. I was lost in his scent, mingled with that of the incense. His fingers slid over my body as if he were imagining me with his touch, his tongue pushing into my mouth. Every part of me opened to his exploration, parts I'd never touched myself and didn't know could feel the way they did. Lovemaking with Hilton was desultory, filled with disinterested touching. I'd never reached an orgasm before, and when I did with Durrell that time the feeling left me weak, grateful toward him for giving me this gift to myself. I lay there, barely conscious of the room, knowing then that I would feel no joy until I could feel him inside me again.

I left them all that day—Hilton, Dani, Rose.

I saw him as often as I could during that next year, lying as I needed with no shame or regret. Everything brought him back to me—the feel of wool when I buttoned Dani's sweater, the scent of incense in a head shop, a glimpse of a full moon because we'd made love one night in moonlight. There was a year of this until I left to be with him.

"Are you sure you want to go through with this?" he asked me when I told him. "Do you want to give up all this to be with me?" I should have read what was really in his eyes that day. Although we talked about it endlessly, he didn't take me seriously until I was standing at his door.

"Yes," I said, because at that point I had nowhere else to go.

Why do you love me?

At the end, he said nothing at all.

In the beginning, he would tell me stories of his childhood. He would tell them lightly as if he were now free of the pain, chuckling over the cruelty of his aunt as if it meant nothing, amusing me with his tales. I sat transfixed, entertained by his words. I'm ashamed now of my detachment, my cool interest in those wounded parts of himself he put on display.

"Have you ever been cold? Have you ever been hungry?" His voice would fill with contempt, but I never heard it then. I would stare at him blankly.

"Have you ever not had a warm coat, or food on the table, or anything you wanted?"

He loved and despised me.

I desired and feared him.

"Forgive me, Durrell," I say to him now when he comes to me at night. What happened between us was inevitable. Our "love" was a suicide pact that only one would survive. Yet we were in it together.

three

These are the last words I said to her:

I need to go, Dani. I just need to go, okay? I love you, baby, okay?

She was wearing her *Electric Company* pajamas because she had taken her bath early so she could watch Rose's TV. I had convinced myself that I'd see her again, that this would not be the last time I would feel her tight, sweet braids against my cheek. She wasn't so much sad as puzzled. Rose knew everything by then. I just didn't know what she would do about it. It was March, a year since the night I met him.

Stupid. Stupid. Stupid. That word is not big enough to tell you what I was.

"Why?" Dani asked.

"I just have to."

I had no choice by then. You create your own hell and I'd sure created mine. Durrell seemed the only way out. I had some silly fantasy about getting the girls in some kind of shared custody agreement with Hilton, bringing Dani to live with us, seeing Rose off to college the following year. In a half-assed way, Durrell had even agreed to go along with it. But there was no way Hilton would ever let that happen. I should have known that.

Dani. Rose. Dani. Rose. Dani. Rose. Dani. Rose.

My talismans against evil. I would whisper their names like prayers.

Danirosedanirosedanirosedanirosedanirosedanirose.

But it wasn't enough to save me.

I made sense to myself when I was with him. I was his student in a way I had never been with Hilton. He was younger than me by a few years, but older in experience. It seemed he knew everything about things I had no idea existed until I met him. It's a cliché, but love always is. I'd fallen in love for the first time in my life. If he'd asked me to drink poison, I would have done it.

Every observation he made seemed wise and sophisticated. He read a lot, so he knew about theater, art, jazz. We'd go to shows because he'd worked with the actors, clubs where he knew the musicians, galleries owned by his rich, slumming friends. Anything that was hip, new, smart Durrell was a part of. I studied everything he did.

Durrell says. Durrell thinks. Durrell knows.

I said those words more often than my name.

"What the hell do I care what that fool says?" Trish finally asked me when she saw me. It was weeks before she returned my calls, and when she did she was distant and judgmental. She'd dropped by the office where I was working on her way home. I'd lost weight, and that was the first thing she noticed.

"You look like shit."

"Thanks for telling me."

She lit a cigarette and watched me without saying anything. A sad smile formed on her face and she shook her head. "The very sound of that man's name rolling out your mouth like it does every ten minutes makes me want to throw up, do you realize that?" This was a Trish I didn't know, a bitter, contemptuous one. She gazed around the office, avoiding my eyes. It belonged to a physician, an internist, who was a friend of the producer of his first film. I worked three days a week as a receptionist. I didn't make much money, just enough to keep me in cigarettes and get my hair done so I could tell myself that I wasn't totally dependent upon him, not enough to leave when things got bad. But they weren't bad yet, not on the day I spoke to Trish.

"So how do you like your job?"

"Okay."

She settled down in the chair next to me, leaning her leather briefcase on the edge of the desk.

"I'm sorry, Maria."

"For what?

"I feel responsible for the mess I think you've made of your life. For Durrell. For losing the girls."

"Well, Durrell—" I stopped short, avoiding her eyes. "I'm okay, other than working in this shitty job and missing my kids. Hilton won't let me get anywhere near them. I keep hoping they'll show up on my doorstep. I left the address with Dani when I left, so she'd have something written down, so she'd know where I was."

"You haven't heard from them?"

"No. He's changed the number to an unlisted one. He changed the door locks, too. I went over one day when he was at work."

"They're your kids. He may not have agreed with what you did, but he can't keep them from you. Have you seen a lawyer?"

"No."

"Why not?"

"Things are just too, well, unsettled. I will when things get calmer."

"I have a friend, Lisa Bonavera. She does pro bono work for one of my women's groups. She's a nice woman. Smart. Give her a call as soon as you can." Trish jotted down her number on a piece of paper and gave it to me. She didn't stay much longer, and when she got up to leave, she wouldn't look me in the eye. "Call me if you need to talk," was all she said.

I promised I would but didn't until the end. She knew more about him than I did, and I didn't want to face it.

By June, I'd begun to notice the cracks. I knew his stories by heart, and since he never told the same one twice I assumed most of them were lies. I knew when he was being cute or cunning and that he smiled the widest at people he despised. I was becoming immune to him, and he knew it.

His offhand remarks were harmless at first, at least they seemed so. The snide asides about my taste in music or books, the TV shows I liked. The fact that I laughed too loud or not enough, that my shoes made too much noise when I walked or walked too soft, sneaking upon him like a thief. He didn't like that I couldn't catch my breath after sex. Or I panted so loud the whole damn building could hear me. He talked about women he knew, had known, wanted to know. Why couldn't I be like this one with her short, pert smile or that one with her degree from Spelman or Barnard, the one with wit or big tits. I was too fat, too thin, my breasts too narrow, too flat, my nose too straight, my hair too straight, my lips too straight. My skin too light, like a fucking ghost, he said.

"Go back to your life," he told me late in June. "There is nothing left between us."

I had no life to go back to.

When we made love there was no feeling; he fucked me, that was what we did by then.

"Why do you put up with it? You left Hilton. You can leave him. Go back to the girls," Trish said when I let the truth slip out.

She had taken me to dinner, a Chinese restaurant a block and a half from where I lived. I hadn't seen Durrell in two days. I was desperate and lonely, so I swallowed my pride and called her.

"What did you get from him anyway?" She took a sip of wine, studied me over the rim of the glass.

"I got myself."

"That's bullshit, and you know it."

But it wasn't at first. I saw myself through his eyes. He was the only person who I thought had really ever seen me. Not my mother, who saw herself, or Hilton, who saw what he wanted to see. I lived in the memory of that first year that I met Durrell, my fantasy of what I thought had been between us. I imagined I could bring it back—if I were understanding enough, smart enough, looked good enough. What I felt for him had to be worth the price I had paid. I had to believe that.

But I had also begun to sense his disgust. The weight of what I'd done had fallen on him, too. He hadn't deceived me; I was as guilty as he was.

"Do you remember who you were?" Trish asked. "Do you remember who you were when we were girls, before this shit went down, before him, before Hilton, even before the girls? Grab ahold of that, Maria, and keep it inside you."

"It's gone, Trish. I gave it up."

"Then you really are lost," Trish said, her eyes dropping to her plate.

I took a gulp of tea, focused on the cup, not feeling how hot it was and that it scalded my mouth.

"Did he ever threaten you, beat you, rape you?" asked Lisa Bonovera. Trish called her for me after they'd taken me to jail. She was a good woman, a serious feminist when that was still the thing to be. She took my case pro bono. Came to see me in prison. Tried to fight Hilton for my girls, even though we both knew it was too late then. Did everything she could to make things better. But in the end it did no good.

"If he beat you, you could call it self-defense. You shot him once. A lucky shot. Maybe you didn't really mean to kill him, and if you did it was in anger for past abuse, in self-defense. Increasingly, that is recognized as an excuse for women who kill abusive men, especially if it was over a number of years."

"But I was only with him for six months. I left my children for him in March and killed him in September."

"You've got to give me something to work with, Mariah. "Exactly why did you kill him? He must have done something to bring it on."

I studied my hands, how I'd bitten my nails to the quick again.

"You're not telling me something, Mariah. You're holding something back. Why won't you tell me what happened that day?"

"I've told you all I can," I said. "He never hit me as such," I added.

"What do you mean, 'as such'?"

"Just what I said."

"Look, there's only one of you alive to tell it. Tell it the way you want to tell it so you can get your life back, see your kids again. Maybe you'll have a chance to beat this."

But I couldn't bring myself to tell it all. There was no way I was going to tell it.

"He must have beaten you!" she said.

"He never beat me physically."

"Emotionally?"

"I guess you could call it that."

"And sex. Was there ever any incident of rape?"

"There were times he wanted to do it and I

didn't, but that became a game between us. I didn't know where my wanting him began or ended."

She shook her head with sympathy and disgust.

The truth was, Durrell's touch had become a weapon, yet I couldn't stop wanting it. I couldn't fully admit to myself how bad things had gotten between us.

Until Elias Belle. I didn't tell her about Elias Belle. I was too ashamed for that.

He was a kid I worked with, early twenties, much younger than me. Our names were almost the same, Belle, Dell, as he liked to point out, so he thought we should be friends and that was what we became. He worked Tuesdays and Thursdays, I came in on Mondays and Wednesdays; we were together on Fridays. Me answering phones, him filing folders. I looked forward to Fridays, because I would see him, the only person I knew who had no connection to Durrell.

He was boyishly handsome, bright smile, long lashes that reminded me of Rose's, dimple in his chin. Good build but rangy, the kind of body he would grow into if trouble never met him, and I was trouble but neither of us knew it yet.

He was innocent when it came to sex. Maybe he'd done it a couple of times with Lena, his girlfriend in high school, and once or twice after that. Not all that much for somebody his age. We talked about sex a lot. Half the time he was trying to shock me in some silly schoolboy attempt to turn me on, more amusing than insulting. I knew he had a crush on me and was flattered because it was so obvious. In an odd way, I had one on him, too. I wasn't sure where to put him, though. He was too old to be like a son, not quite old enough to be anything else. Closer to a younger brother maybe.

He'd bring me coffee Friday mornings. Exotic brews you hear about now because of Starbucks—Kenyan, Costa Rican, Jamaican Blue Mountain. Elias was ahead of his times in that way. He'd bring scones, too, blueberry, raspberry, tasty ones picked up at Balducci's on his way to work. I'd never had scones before, and it delighted him to introduce me to new things. We'd go out to lunch some days, Indian restaurants where we'd heap our plates full of curries, samosas, tandoori chicken. I'd never had Indian food before. Durrell hated it, so I'd never tried it and I found that I loved it. Elias reminded me of who I had been before—the Maria that Trish had mentioned. He brought me back the part that belonged to my girls—the funny, protective, caring piece I'd forgotten was in me, but mixed with a harmless dash of flirtation.

He wanted to become an architect and was headed to some school down South after he finished junior college. He loved to sketch, never came to work without a pad, always drawing something. It made me laugh, how his hands were constantly at work. He sketched me once or twice. For years, I kept his drawings. I'm not sure what became of them.

It was only a matter of time before Durrell got curious. Not jealous, he made that clear since we were supposed to have an "open" relationship, secure enough to let other people into our lives, but he did all the letting.

So he wanted to meet this kid, this Elias I kept talking about, and he stopped by the office, charmed Elias like he did everybody else who landed in his web. A couple weeks after they met, I found out they had begun to hang out together, and the days Elias wasn't with me he was with Durrell.

"Smart kid. He should get around more," Durrell told me one night. His interest in Elias made me uncomfortable. I knew I should warn him, but he'd met Durrell through me, so what the hell could I say?

That was 1979, my summer of drugs. I'd missed the sixties and made up for lost time— snorting, smoking, drinking, anything I could get my hands on to ease my pain. Rum. Acid. Cocaine. Peyote. Hashish. Opium once. Bourbon, a salute to Durrell's Southern roots. Marijuana, of course. For breakfast, lunch, dinner. We were high on something all the time. Whatever we could get. Maybe that was why things happened as they did.

"I think your friend must be a virgin," Durrell told me one Saturday morning. "I think he digs you, why don't you fuck him?"

I ignored him. He was high, and I'd drunk too much the night before and still felt sick. I was doing the dishes. The place was stinking hot. We were low on cash, and Durrell was bugging me to go into the little bit of money my mother had left me, which I'd made the mistake of mentioning the week before. I didn't feel like any shit from him. He was smiling when he said it, and that scared me.

"No, really, I think you should fuck him, have a good time with him. He's a nice kid, you'd do him a favor."

"Leave him alone, Durrell." There was a knife lying on the kitchen table. He must have seen me glance at it because he moved toward me fast, knocked it off the table onto the floor. Later that day, he started up again, lit a cigarette, blew his words out with the smoke.

"No, really, I think it would do him some good. Maybe you, too."

"And that wouldn't bother you, would it?"

"Nope. You know, maybe it's time you fucked

somebody besides me and that asshole you were married to. Do the boy some good. I told him he could fuck you if he wanted."

I slapped him hard across his face. "Don't ever say that to me again," I said. He looked surprised, but that was it. He left it alone for a week or so, and I thought he'd forgotten it. I made myself forget it because there was a part of me that found Elias attractive, too. But I didn't want to think about that.

The three of us would get together on Fridays after work. At first it was good having somebody to talk to beside Durrell. Elias was *my* friend, not his, but I began to notice the way Durrell's name was creeping into his conversation. *Durrell* was the authority. *Durrell* was the standard bearer. It was like Trish had noticed it in me.

Elias's older brother had been killed the summer before in a car accident. He'd shown me a photograph of him, and he resembled Durrell— same sleepy eyes, same curl of the lips—and I knew then what drew Elias to him. Durrell could sniff out the hurt in wounded people. He'd smelled it in me; he smelled it in Elias.

It was a Friday night in July. The windows had been locked all day because somebody had broken into the building the week before. When the three of us got home, everything was sweating— the windows, the walls, the furniture, me, Durrell, Elias. There was too much heat to breathe. We opened the windows even though there was no breeze, smoked some hash, sat on the fire escape, drank some beer, did some coke, drank some wine.

I hadn't eaten since lunch. I was dizzy, so I went into the bathroom to shower and get cool. I still remember how good the water felt hitting my body. I'd bought some soap the week before that smelled like lemons. Sweet Sour Lemon it was called, and the lather made me feel fresh and clean. To this day, the smell of lemons makes me sick. I stayed in the shower a long time, washing my hair with the soap, letting the water run down my back, over my face, feeling the cool creep over me and the smell seep into my body. I was tired and still drunk, and when I got out of the shower I wrapped towels around my hair and body, stumbled into the bedroom, fell into the bed.

I woke up between them.

This is what I remember: Durrell's drunken laughter as he shoved his dick into me. Him coming out, then pushing Elias between my legs. Their hands all over me, pulling, stroking, pinching, scratching. How thin Elias was, how vulnerable and small, like some lost, scared kid. I remember his throat and shoulders on my palms. His smooth, hairless chest against my breasts and tongue. Durrell's hands jamming hard inside me.

Someone's fingers tugging at me, mouth snatching at my breast, teeth biting into my thighs, and when I opened my eyes seeing Elias. There was nothing in his face. Not disgust, certainly not pleasure, and I tried to tell him I was sorry, but I couldn't move my mouth. It was heavy and dead. No words came out. I closed my eyes, blacked out smells, sound, flesh, taste, and when I opened them Elias was gone. All I felt was shame. Mine and his. I never saw him again.

I threw what I could into a suitcase and left Durrell that morning and went to Trish.

"You were raped," Trish told me. "The bastards gang-raped you!"

I couldn't look her in the eye. She grabbed my head, turned it toward her, made me look at her. "It's not your shame, it's his. And that other little son of a bitch."

"We pulled him into our craziness. I did, Trish. I corrupted him."

"Seems to me there was more than enough corruption to go around," she said with a sour smile. "It never occurred to me before, but I think my man Durrell must be a faggot. He must have had a thing for Elias. If a man gets into a threesome, it's with two women, not another dude. It would have been with you and one of those countless chicks he talks about, not some dumb kid. He wanted to fuck the boy himself. You were there for cover. He's obviously got a thing for boys. And innocence, too. He likes spoiling untouched things. Like the kid. Like you."

"I don't think Durrell is a homosexual."

"Whatever he is, you better get the hell away from him. Stay here until you get on your feet. Save some money. We can figure out a way to force Hilton to let you have your girls. They always give the kids to the mother. Everything will be okay."

She hugged me tight like I used to hold my daughters.

"Don't worry, Maria. All bad things pass. You just have to endure them until they're gone. Sooner or later shining times will find you, too!"

"Shining times! What the hell are you talking about?" I felt like she was making light of my situation, and that made me mad.

"Shining times are the opposite of shitty ones, and you've had your share of those. Sooner or later some sunshine is going to break through. Things will get better. I promise they will."

And for the next few weeks, it seemed like maybe Trish was right, that things would be better, that some sunshine might be coming my way. Until I went back to Durrell's place to get the rest of my things.

What ever became of Elias Belle? How many Fridays ago was that? So many I can't count them. Is he the architect he wanted to become? Has he forgiven himself and me for what happened that night? I've forgiven us both.

I finish my second drink and read Hilton Dell's obituary again. I will go tomorrow. Just once more I have to see them. I need to hold Dani close to me again, beg forgiveness of my Rosie for the part I played. Then I will know that things turned out all right, that they weren't destroyed by all that I did, and I will find some peace in this hell I created.

Dani

four

"**O**pen the door so you can see what's behind it." Those were the words my father said to me on the Wednesday morning that he died. It's Friday now, and I haven't been able to cry.

His voice was loud and clear that day even though he hadn't spoken in a week. I had no idea what he was talking about. I pulled up the sheets he'd kicked off and tucked them around his shoulders, then touched his lips with ice chips, which the doctor said he'd want instead of water near the end. My husband, Chance, fed them to me when I was in labor with our son, Teddy. Ice chips—good for birthing and dying.

"The door is open, Father, and there is nothing behind it." My voice was gentle, but "Father" made it seem harsh because it's such an old-fashioned word. When I was a kid, I used to call him "Daddy," but I haven't said that in years. "Father" suited him better because it was stern and aloof like him. Ben laughed the first time he heard me say it.

"Father? Dani, I don't believe you call your old man 'Father.' Nobody says that anymore, not even rich-ass white folks. It doesn't even *sound* black," he said, stroking the small of my back with his elegant fingers.

It was inappropriate to think about my lover sitting with my dying father, but Ben was always on my mind. Just the thought of him brought back that old familiar thrill, followed by my old familiar guilt.

"Open the door, Maria." My father opened his eyes and gazed at me. I knew he saw my mother's face in mine. I look like her, but I'm the same dark brown color as my father. My sister, Rose, looks like him except for her color, which she got from my mother. My aunt would say Rose was the color of café au lait with too much cream. Rose and I have always suspected that our mother's skin color was one of the things my aunt held against her.

As Eskimos are said to have a dozen names for ice and snow, my Aunt Lucille has a dozen ways to classify somebody by skin color. Ebony, teak, mahogany, oak—those terms are for men. The ones for women are food. Skinned almond would be the way she'd describe my mother, almond *sans* skin.

How many times had my father looked at me and cursed my mother under his breath? I asked Rose that one afternoon when we were both grown enough to hash out the sorrow that was our childhood.

"If he does it, it's not deliberate," Rose explained, her eyes soft with empathy. My sister has the kindest eyes of anyone I know. They're big and round like a doe's, with lashes so long people envy her. Bambi eyes. If I look hard, I can see my father's face in hers, the one that was there before the bitterness took hold. "He's been through a lot, Dani. Don't forget what happened to him."

"The door is open, Father," I said. *And Maria is gone.*

"Open the door!" I was surprised by the strength of his voice, as if he'd been saving it up for the last day. What door was he talking about, anyway? This room was too damned big for him to see any door that was open or closed. His bedroom took up the whole third floor of this dreary-ass house where he'd lived since I was born. Maybe it was the door to life he wanted opened.

"How's he doing?" Rose came into the room and rested her hand on my shoulder.

"The same," I said, even though I sensed he was getting worse.

"Listen, babe, I got to get to school." "Babe" is what Rose calls me sometimes. I *was* her babe when Mariah up and left. "McCafferty is bringing in some state people this morning, a definite pain in the ass, but he pointedly told me to have my big butt there when they come." She kissed the top of my head. "You okay?"

"As good as him." I nodded toward the bed.

"Dani, that's not funny!"

"I didn't mean it to be funny. It's the truth."

She bent down low and whispered, "Hold on till I get home, you hear me, Pop? Hold on! You know how much I love you. I know you do." She stood up with a groan. Her back hurts her these days, along with her knees and ankles. She complains about them like an old woman, even though she's just nine years older than me. She gained fifty pounds when our mother went to jail, and she's still heavy.

"Do you really love him?"

"Yes, I do, and you do, too. You just don't know it yet. Are you sure you're okay?"

"Don't worry about me, I'll call your cell if anything changes. Where's Aunt Lucille?"

"Downstairs drinking coffee. I told her to go back to bed, but you know how she is. She doesn't need to see this."

"She's tougher than him."

"She's not as tough as you think, believe me."

"If he gets any worse—"

"It's already worse."

"You know what I mean, if—"

"Yeah." No need to state the obvious.

We watched him in silence.

"Why the hell couldn't he just go to a hospital, like everybody else does, like somebody with good sense?"

"Because Hilton Dells is not like everybody else," I said. My neck and shoulders were tight, as if I'd worked out all night. I hadn't realized I'd been sitting here that long. "He asked for her."

Rose stiffened. "Maria?" she asked even though she knew by the tone of my voice who I was talking about.

"Mariah," I corrected her. Before she left, my mother told me to call her Mariah. It was the name I read in the newspapers, which they tried to hide from me, and the one reporters said on TV. It was the name kids threw in my face when they teased me about her at school.

"Mommy" or "Mariah" to me. "Maria" to Rose. "Maria-who-called-herself-Mariah" to my Aunt Lu, who never called her anything else.

"What did he say?"

"He told her to open the door."

"What door? I just walked through it."

"Hell if I know. He's not making sense."

"It's been a long night, Dani, and he's dying. He's not supposed to make any sense. Have you called Chance?"

"No, not yet." Sometimes I wonder if Rose is secretly in love with my husband. They look out for each other, playfully ganging up on me. She saw him first, if that means anything, but then handed him down to me as generously as she did her old dolls and cashmere sweaters. As far as I know, there has never been a man in Rose's life. For all I know, she may still be a virgin, although I hope not. Sex is something Rose doesn't discuss with me. In that way, she's a very private person, although we've talked about everything else— from drugs to death. If she's ever had a lover, she's never told me about him. Those nine years between us make a difference; she still thinks I'm a kid.

"Call him, Dani. He should know what is going on. He has to tell everybody at work. They'll want to do some big thing or another. A founder's memorial—" She stopped, not wanting to finish it.

"Okay." I hugged her and felt the warmth and protection from her I always did.

"Love you, babe."

"Love you, too."

She glanced at our father as she left the room. "The door *is* open, Hilton Dells," she said as if reprimanding one of her novice teachers or a naughty eighth-grader.

After Rose left, I placed more ice chips between his lips. He closed his mouth tight, determined not to take them. He reminded me of my little boy, and I touched his cheek the way I do my son's.

"Damn you, Maria," he said, and I pulled my hand away fast, taking back any tenderness I felt.

I wish I were like Rose. She is all-forgiving, the selfless one with enough good inside her for anybody who needs a dose of kindness. She loses herself daily in the lives of the needy children in her school and the young teachers she mentors. Everyone loves and admires her because she gives herself so completely.

But I'm Dani, the baby of the family, the flawed, spoiled one. Sometimes I think I am selfish to my core, like some spiteful little beast with sharp teeth and nasty claws, determined to get her way. I used to be proud of that, used to call it my survivor's instinct, but I'm not sure about that anymore. To be honest, I'm not sure about much of anything anymore. There are days I look in the mirror and don't know who I am.

My father hadn't said my mother's name to me in more than ten years. I remember because I was twenty the last time he said it. I'd told him I was going to marry Chance, who was twenty-two, and as eager as me to make a commitment. My father looked at me as if I were crazy.

"Why in the hell would you want to do something stupid like that?" he said. I was used to him dashing my plans with a raised eyebrow or dismissive laugh, and I'd geared myself up for this confrontation. His face is long, narrow, and full-featured like a Nigerian mask. When he is mad or disgusted his nostrils flare, which they did that day.

"Because I love him."

"Love, Dani? You don't know what you're talking about."

I stood my ground. "Yes, I do. I love Chance and he loves me, and I'm going to marry him no matter what you say."

"Love means nothing. It's nothing at all."

"How could you say that?"

"Maria was twenty when I married her. Twenty years old." He shook his head as if dislodging an unpleasant memory. "You should learn from her mistake."

"What should I learn? *You* were the old one. You were the *old* fool who should have known better." My tone would have earned me a slap when I was younger, but now just got me that look, the one that could turn me to shit. It was the truth, and we both knew it, but this was the first time I had thrown in his face what had happened between him and my mother.

So he reluctantly gave us his blessing, and I married Chancellor Carter, and my father grew to love him like the son he never had because they were made of the same stuff—a head for business that put folks in their place, a gift for making money, stealing power. Maybe that was why I'd been attracted to Chance in the first place, maybe that was why I fell in love with him. But Chance seemed different from my father. No one, after all, is exactly the same as somebody else.

I wonder sometimes, though, if I'm not the same as Mariah, if her past will be my future.

When my father said my mother's name that day, his voice had been neutral, as if he said it all the time, as if she wasn't an unmentionable. My Aunt Lucille said her name more often. *Maria-who-called-herself-Mariah* she'd spit out as if it were a curse. Maria-who-called-herself-Mariah, who shamed us, dirtied our name, spurned her brother's generosity, scoffed at his manhood. My Aunt Lu, whom I adore and often dislike within the same thirty seconds, raised us when my mother left. She did it with a heavy hand that found no resistance and a temper that I've discovered in myself. I'm still recovering from her particular brand of rage and love. I have never been able to think of her as my mother, and I know that must hurt her. I have saved that space for my real one. Mommy-Maria-Mariah.

But my Aunt Lu does love me, especially considering the circumstances under which she came into our lives. She had settled into her single life before she came to live with us, independent, pretty "fly," as she used to call herself. In her old photographs, she's a confident woman in her late thirties, primed to do anything she damned well pleased anytime she felt like it. She had her own "pad," as she used to call her place in the Village, which was rare for a black woman in those days, her own car, a couple of lovers whose names she never mentioned. And then suddenly there we were. Her brother's daughters, pining for a woman whom she despised for what she'd done.

I got good stuff from Aunt Lu—a sense of myself as a smart, take-no-nonsense woman who took crap from nobody, least of all those smartass white boys I came up against in college and grad school. She trained me well for that. I have a tough skin; I know how to give as good as I get. I can protect my soft belly so nobody can touch it unless I want them to. I've acquired her tastes, too. A love of Australian red wines and soft French cheese, a passion for Armani suits and Chanel perfumes.

And what did I get from the other, the one who left yet was never gone?

Mommy. Maria. Mariah.

When I was a kid, I whispered her name to myself at night before I fell asleep. When Aunt Lucille would listen to my prayers, I never said it out loud but paused a moment before I started the list of people I wanted to bless, and that was when I said it. Before anybody else. I forgave her for what she'd done, and prayed that God would, too

Mariah Dells is your mother?

I could always tell when the question was coming. I saw it in the curiosity mixed with disgust in their bright little eyes.

"Just say no!" Rose ordered me, with the conviction we'd later hear from Nancy Reagan, her doe eyes filled with the stubborn sense of justice only a teenager can muster. "Just say no! Don't give them the pleasure of embarrassing you!"

"But I'm not embarrassed!"

"You should be!"

"I'm not!" So I would never say it.

"Yeah, she's my mom." I'd add a defiant head toss for good measure, daring somebody to rub it in, eager for a fight, even though I'd never fought anybody in my life. Usually, though, the kid would just stare at me in pity.

Except one kid, I'll never forget him. Mike Raymond, filthy little bastard, straight out of hell. Rose said, in her comforting way, that was just his way of showing he liked me. Eight-year-old boys, she explained, sometimes teased you because they didn't know what else to do.

But I knew better. He was the devil incarnate, and I wished him dead every time I said my prayers. Right after I asked God to forgive Mariah.

And please, God, would you consider letting Mike Raymond enjoy the kingdom of Heaven?

Murdering Mariah. Murdering Mariah. Murdering Mariah. Murdering Mariah. Murdering Mariah. That's your mama. Murdering Mama Mariah.

That was his hellish chant.

Is she like her mother?

The kids I grew up with in my tight, closed world were too polite to ask, but I could read it in the anxious glances of their parents.

Fuck them all!

Yet I was still invited to the birthday parties, debutante balls, Jack and Jill fund-raisers, anywhere and everywhere that the rich black world gathered because my father, after all, was Hilton Dells—founder, CEO, moneymaker, asskicker—of Dells Associates, the oldest, largest, richest black accounting firm in the whole of New Jersey.

No fool like an old fool.

I could read that in their eyes, too. Hell, when I got old enough to know what it meant, I thought it, too.

Hilton Dells had the misfortune of falling in

love with a pretty, silly woman who threw his hard-earned respectability back in his face. Yet who would have thought that such a proper, sweet young thing, mother of two proper, sweet young daughters, was a no-count whore who would betray her husband, abandon her kids, then turn around and shoot her lover a single time through the heart on a Saturday afternoon?

My son Teddy is seven, the same age as me when she left us. He reminds me of myself, same awkwardness and curiosity, same abiding belief in the goodness of life, which I suppose all kids possess until it's snatched away, like it was from me.

I love him more than my life. More than my husband, more than myself. I love him more than I thought I could love anyone. Except her.

On the morning my father died, he opened his eyes, moved his lips, but there were no words this time. For the first time that I'd been there, I could feel his fear as if it were my own. I could sense his sorrow as he slowly let go.

"It's me, Daddy, I love you," I said.

His eyes softened, and I knew this time that he saw me as myself.

"Forgive me, Dani," he said, and then he was gone.

five

After he died, I sat next to him for fifteen minutes, then pulled the blanket up to his chin, the way I do when I tuck in my son. I kissed his cheek, the first time I'd done it in years, the last time I ever would. I could still feel his presence; I made myself feel it. When it wasn't there anymore, I went downstairs and told my aunt that he was gone.

Aunt Lu was sitting in the kitchen where Rose had left her. She wore the green corduroy robe she always did, and her rimless reading glasses were perched on her nose as they always were when she read the morning paper. Everything looked the same, but nothing was or would ever be again. She turned toward me as I entered the room. She knew by my expression what I had to say and slammed her hand over her mouth.

"Oh God! It's over then!" She shook her head as if tossing out some terrible thought, then ran upstairs to his bedroom, her steps wobbling like an old woman's. After she left, I called Dr. Jamison, who had cared for my father since he took ill, and he said he'd be over to take care of everything. He was my father's best friend. He was best man at his wedding, and he was there when Rose and I were born and when our mother left him. They pledged Kappa together at Hampton and twenty-five years later joined the Boulés.

I sat in the kitchen chair for a while, not sure what else to do. I thought about going home but didn't want to see or talk to anybody—not Chance, certainly not Ben, not even Teddy—so I went upstairs to my old room and closed the door.

It's a corner room joined to Rose's old bedroom by a bathroom, which we shared when we were kids. It is an old-fashioned bathroom with a claw-footed tub and a large-basined sink on a pedestal, where I washed my face. I went into my bedroom, stripped down to my underwear, then climbed into bed. The sheets were soft and silky and smelled like Downy, which made me think of my son.

It was early, not quite noon, and the sun poured into my window, which looks out onto our garden. When I was a kid, we had a Jamaican gardener named Bill who grew up in Port Antonio.

He had a gold tooth that lit up his face when he laughed, and large hands with split nails that fascinated me. He taught me how to plant pansies in the spring, impatiens in the summer, and tulips before first frost. He was my first love. My mother and he disappeared around the same time, and at first I thought maybe she'd left with him until Aunt Lucille set me straight. Bad enough she chose the man she did, my aunt muttered, although she didn't go into details then—or later, for that matter. Aunt Lu fired him when she came to live with us. Annuals were a waste of money because they only bloomed one season, she said.

There is some of Bill in Ben, who nurtures dying plants and tends the flowers in his dead wife's garden. Maybe that's why I fell in love with him, because he knows how to care for needy things.

Nothing in my old room has changed. It's still a teenager room, all lavender and white; pink was too conventional for me, even then. The white fake fur rug is worn now and the lacy bed ruffles and drooping canopy are frayed. The half-used bottles of perfume are where I left them standing years ago. Shalimar, Norell, my aunt's Chanel #5. The room has always had a musty damp smell. When I was a teenager I burned incense to cover it and hide the smell of the weed I smoked whenever I could get it.

Everything ached now, even my mind. Especially my mind. I lay on the bed and listened to the sounds of the house like I used to do when I was a kid. The walls creaking for no reason, the water draining through ancient pipes. I used to listen for my mother, waiting for her to come back to me, my hands folded like I was begging or praying.

I tried again to cry for my father but couldn't, so I thought about the other one, whose soul he said I have. Had she buried her spirit deep inside me, biding her time until she could break loose and lead me into hell? I'd gone ten years without thinking about her, wondering what had become of her, then he'd ordered her to open that damned door and now I couldn't get her out of my mind.

My mother had been gone for years by the time my room turned into this lavender-and-white teenage fantasy. Each piece of furniture, each lacy pillow sham and dust ruffle pushed her further away. I abandoned her with the other remnants of my childhood, which was the surest way to show I was a teenager like Rose. My grief turned to anger and finally to shame; I joined the ranks of the grown-ups. Mommy became Mariah.

I had stopped writing her letters years before. At first I sent them to the address she had given me the night she left, the one of the apartment she shared with Durrell Alexander. She'd shoved it into my hand in her hurry to escape before my father got home. "Here is where I'll be if you need me," she'd said, and I believed her. That was what I told her in my letters, scribbled with a turquoise pencil because that was her favorite color. After she murdered him, I sent them to the prison where the newspaper said they took her: Mariah Dells c/o Somerset Women's House of Detention. The guards probably had a good laugh about that or maybe just felt sorry for the kid who didn't know how to find her mother.

She never wrote me back. She abandoned me like she had our father, choosing Durrell Alexander, even in death, over Rose and me. So I decided everything people said about her was true.

The woman I *thought* I knew never really existed, the one with the quirky grin and crooked teeth, who drew pictures on my arm, told me and Rose stories, made vanilla milk for us before we went to bed. The one who wore copper earrings, laughed at my jokes, and sprayed me with her rose cologne when I closed my eyes, actually lived next door to the Tooth Fairy and Mrs. Claus. She was imagined, a childhood fantasy. Someone to drop from my life when the appropriate age came around.

I hardened myself against her. I pushed her face, touch, voice, smell away. It made me sick and dizzy to remember her; it hurt my stomach to smell her cologne; the very memory of her frightened me. I had Rose, my Aunt Lu, and my father, more or less, to fill the hole she left. *We* were family, like that Sister Sledge song that came out the year she left. *We are family.*

But I could still lose myself in the memory of the way my room looked before she left. The corner where my Barbie dollhouse sat—Christy, the black Barbie, and her technicolor Ken perched on their plastic couch, pretty and content in their plastic universe (like me and Chance these days). My Easy Bake oven and Sesame Street sheets in their orange, green, and yellow splendor. I found my doll in all her glamorous regalia recently and that whole year came back to me. I could smell her perfume.

I caught a whiff of her scent recently in a store walking down the aisle. I was looking for Advil and someone sprayed a tester of it, and I stopped dead in my tracks, as if I'd lost my way. They call it Evelyn Rose now, but I don't remember that being the name then. Did she name my sister after her favorite flower? That's something she would have done. She was a dreamer who burned cookies, left doors unlocked, intended to do this or that, and never did anything except read us fairy tales and tell us stories.

"Our mother is such a space cadet," Rose would say with a roll of her eyes and a suck of her teeth. "Mom, grow up!" she would scold her. Rose, the adult to our mother's wayward child.

I'm in a similar state these days—burning toast, forgetting groceries in carts, leaving important items in ridiculous places. So she *must* have been in love with him, I'll grant her that. I'm sure she was when she left with him that night.

It was a Thursday. I remember that because *What's Happening!!* was on TV, and I was in seventh heaven. Rerun was my favorite character, because he could dance so well, but I liked his sister Dee, too, who was always saying, "Oooh, I'm going to tell Mama," which cracked me up even though I'd heard it a thousand times. I'd say it to Rose at least half a dozen times a day, which got on her nerves and made me double over in laughter.

I was lying on Rose's bed. Rose had saved her money and bought herself a small TV, which was one of her treasures. She'd let me watch it when she wasn't home. Rose was the most popular girl in her class, president of this and that, never without a date. She's always been pretty, and she was especially so then. Occasionally she even modeled clothes in one of the stores that catered to teenagers. "Dream Girl" was what her friends used to call her, although unlike our mother, Rose was practical, living in the here and now; that hasn't left her. I don't remember where she was that night.

My mother came into the room and sat on the bed. I must have looked up and grinned, settling closer, because she put her arm around me, hugged me tight.

"Danielle, I've got something important to tell you." Nobody called me that. Dani was the only name I knew; that should have tipped me off that something was up. But I didn't get it then, and not for months later.

"I've got something important to tell you."

I must have laughed then, Rerun was up to his bullshit, so I didn't respond, but she took my hand, and she rarely did that. I saw that she was crying.

"What's wrong, Mommy?"

"I have to tell you something."

"What?" I started to cry then, too, because her tears frightened me, so she made herself smile. I tried to smile then, too.

"Dani." Back to the familiar. "I have to leave tonight for a while."

"Where are you going? The stores are closed!"

"I'm not going to the store." She stopped then. I remember that because she tipped her head to the side as if she were thinking about something; she did that when she was worried.

"Are you going to the park?" That was our special place down the street from our house. Each season was magical. Gray squirrels and golden leaves in fall. Icy hanging branches in winter. Cherry blossoms and tulips in spring, and roses, her favorite, in summer. Even now, I go there to find peace. I hoped she'd take me there, even though I knew it was late.

"I have to live somewhere else for a while. I need for you to know that I love you, and I'm not leaving because of you."

"Where are you going?"

She heard the panic in my voice because she grabbed me again, pulled me to her; her fuzzy sweater tickled my cheek. It was my favorite sweater. A red angora one that Rose and I had given her for Christmas the year before; Rose picked it out.

"I can't tell you now, but I will." I pulled away. Angry.

"Why?"

She didn't answer then and never did. "When things settle down, when everything is better, I'll come to see you and you can come to see me, too. And we will live together then."

"Live together where?" I was skeptical. Funny, I didn't ask about my father. I must have known even then. "Why are you leaving?" That was the *real* question.

She ripped a page from one of Rose's notebooks and printed an address on it. She folded it into a tiny square and gave it to me.

"Here is where I'll be if you need me. I'll be in touch with you when I move again. Then you can come to see me, okay?"

"No!"

"I need to go, Dani. I just need to go, okay?"

That was what she needed to hear, that it was okay. Right. That's what you say to a kid when you tell her something that's *not* going to be okay. Like a kid is supposed to give you some kind of approval for something. Like it's up to the kid. Hell, I say it to Teddy all the time. Like *he's* the adult and I'm the kid. Like it's *his* decision.

No, Mommy. It wasn't okay because I never heard from your lying, cheating ass again. Okay?

She didn't look like she was going anywhere that night. She had on jeans with the red sweater and sneakers, blue Keds with the funny socks with valentines I'd given her for Mother's Day. And the rose perfume that for the rest of my life would bring her back to me. She hugged me again, like she couldn't get enough of me. Then she said it was time for me to go to bed, and she wanted to tuck me in, but she kept glancing at her watch.

It was my father's club night, and he got in late, around eleven-thirty usually. I'm sure he was the last man on earth she wanted to see. So she watched me brush my teeth, listened to me say my prayers, sat on the edge of the bed until I fell asleep.

By the next morning, I'd forgotten what she told me. I ran to her room, searching for her like I always did. My father was sitting on the bed. He was dressed for work in his dark gray suit and silk tie, his shoes polished to their usual shine, his gold watch sparkling on his wrist. He wasn't moving. He held his head in his hands, like it hurt. He didn't look at me when I came into the room.

"Where's Mommy?" He stared at me as if he didn't know who I was, and at that point I must have remembered what she'd told me because I ran into her closet, tripped over his shoes. I threw open the closet door, then started to laugh. It was a nightmare. Her clothes were still there. I could smell her perfume so she was downstairs fixing breakfast. Pancakes because it was early. Or maybe waffles, the kind I liked with bananas.

"She's not here," he said.

"Where is she?"

"Gone."

I didn't believe him.

"Mommy!" I ran to the top of the stairs. My heart was pounding by then. I still remember how scared I was, like I was going to throw up, like I wouldn't be able to stop. I called out to her again, then ran.

"Stop that noise!"

I ran into the closet. Maybe she was hiding like she did sometimes when we played. I searched for her, pulling her clothes on top of me: the off-shoulder turquoise sheath she wore to parties, the flannel robe that smelled like bacon, the red and yellow blouses, corduroy pants, woolen suits all hung so neatly on their hangers. I pulled them down, touching, screaming, smelling her.

"Stop it!" my father said.

"Where's Mommy?"

"Didn't I tell you to stop it!" He yanked me out of her closet. He grabbed my arm hard, and I squealed in pain. He was mad, and I didn't know if it was at me or her. But I was mad, too, so it didn't matter. I ran out of their room, slamming the door behind me.

Even though it was a school day, Rose was still in bed. When I ran into her room, she pulled the blanket up over her head, and then peeked out and I crawled in beside her. I curled up into the gentle contours of her body, her down comforter covered us both. I moved as close as I could to her, feeling her warmth like I always did, hearing her breath. One of the romance novels she liked to read fell on the floor.

"Damn her. Damn her. Damn her. Damn her. Damn her to hell!" she said.

"Stop it. Rose. Don't say that about Mommy," I wailed, and she stopped, protecting me then like she always did.

"Did she say anything to you last night, Dani?" Her voice was hoarse but controlled.

"She said she was leaving."

"Did she tell you where she was going?"

I gave Rose the paper with the address written on it. She copied it down for herself and tucked it into her jewelry box where she kept her treasures, then gave it back to me.

"Don't tell Daddy," I said. Even then I must have known it was a secret.

"I won't, Dani, but please don't cry. Don't cry!"

But I couldn't stop. She held me until I quieted down.

"It will be okay," she said. "I'll find a way to make it okay."

Sometime that day, my father threw out my mother's clothes. I went to her closet before I went to bed that night. None of her was left. Her closet, with its shelves and cubicles and hidden secret places for scarves, stockings, and underwear, smelled like Lysol. The fancy gold leaf paper had been stripped off the shelves. Even the hangers, the pretty ones with silk where she hung her sweaters, were gone. He'd rid himself of her, scrubbed her out.

Except for the brooch.

It lay in a corner on the floor of her closet. They had both missed it. It was the kind of brooch you pin on a severe dark suit to give it style, although it wasn't elegant, not like the other jewelry he bought her, which was subtle and low-key, but flamboyant with large fake pearls shaped into a flower. I slipped it into my pocket, then hid it in my Barbie jewelry box.

He always bought her jewelry; she never picked anything out. He used to tell her she had no taste. When I had a cold once and couldn't taste fruit, he told me my "taste" was gone, so I thought that was what he meant. My mother had no taste, and neither did I.

I don't know what legal maneuvers he took to "protect" us from her and Durrell Alexander. Rose told me years later that she'd tried to see us. She'd come over on my father's late night, but all the locks had been changed. She should have known that much about him, that that would be the first thing he would do. But she was a dreamer like everybody said, so maybe it simply didn't occur to her. Rose said she found a note from her that had been thrown in the trash, but didn't read it. I don't think that was the truth.

I kept a pink "Dear Diary" with a black Barbie on the cover, which I recently found. As a historian, I have an academic interest in what events transpired during those months, and it would have been interesting to know what I was feeling, what I was going through. Most of the pages were blank, though, and the rest were filled with non-sense: goings-on at school, who liked who in my class. Rerun and Dee, Mork and Mindy. There was nothing about what had happened to my family.

My father did what had to be done. He had us and he had the power, and he wasn't about to let her anywhere near us. And then came my Aunt Lucille, as pissed as he was at this wayward tramp, whom she'd warned him against but whom he married anyway, abandoning her, her advice, and his good sense along with it. And now he had been abandoned. Served him right.

She took things firmly in hand, fired Bill the gardener, hired Lil the housekeeper, who is with her still and probably responsible for my sheets smelling of Downy today. She bought our school clothes at Saks, got braces to straighten my teeth so "they wouldn't look like *hers*." She scolded our teachers, corrected our homework, cared for us with diligence and good humor. I sometimes sensed her resentment: the cross words that came from nowhere, the cigarettes chain-smoked in the middle of the night, Miles Davis wailing in the background. But any bitterness she felt waned as we grew older, and there's peace between us now. A solemn, occasionally quarrelsome, loving peace.

But it is my mother's voice that comes out when I speak to my son; her jokes are the ones I tell him. It was Mariah's brooch I tucked close to my breast on my wedding day.

six

*W*e will bury my father tomorrow. The four of us sit at the kitchen table in his home, and speak in low voices as if he can hear us. Rose and Lucille are at one end, like Mama and Papa, me and Chance on either side like kids. Lucille reads with reverence the copy of his will he'd given her when he got sick. There are no surprises. He is to be cremated three days after his death, which will be on Saturday. His ashes are to be buried next to his parents in a local cemetery. He wants a memorial service held on the same day. He wants it to be held in the lobby of his building. The service can last no more than an hour.

Even from the grave, he is controlling us.

"Does anybody mind?" Lucille pulls out the pack of Winstons and the gold-plated lighter she keeps in her sweater. My aunt has been a smoker for as long as I can remember, but never smoked in front of us. My father used to tell her she'd be dead of lung cancer by the time she was fifty. She's outlived his prediction.

He left everything to me and Rose—the house, the business, his brand-new Lincoln Town Car. Lucille isn't mentioned at all, but if she's angry about being left out of his will, she doesn't show it. This is yet another thing for me to hold against my father, another example of how small and mean he could be.

"What a selfish bastard he was," I say to Chance later when we are driving home. We have gone fifteen minutes in silence, the masks we wear in front of my family tucked away.

"Don't talk about him that way." Chance speaks sharply, defending him even in death. My father filled in the gaps of "successful" black manhood for my husband in ways that his own deceased father had never been able to. At twenty-two, Chance had wanted to become Hilton Dells—a dark-skinned black man in a nasty white world that sometimes let the light-skinned boys play but held men who looked like him in secret contempt. Chance made no secret of his admiration, and my father fed off it, rewarding him with the lessons that a man like him would teach his heir: how to know good scotch at first sip, play a decent round of golf, cheat fast and sneaky so nobody knew they were conned. He taught him not to trust anyone who didn't look like him, smile in people's face and spit at them when they turned their heads. My father took his side against me when it came to Theresa Arcadia because she was the best thing the company had going for them, and business was more important than a daughter's betrayal. I haven't forgiven him for that, his tacit support of my humiliation.

"He was my father. I can talk about him any way I want to."

Silence. Chance stares ahead. I start again. "He was selfish not to leave Lucille anything. I can't believe it. Son of a bitch!"

"Don't call your father names like that, Dani. What the hell is wrong with you? Let the man rest in peace, for Christ's sake. I know you and Hil had your issues—"

"That's not the half of it."

"You're talking about Theresa Arcadia, aren't you?" His hands tighten around the steering wheel.

"What do you think?"

"Let's not go there, please. Not today. How many times do I have to tell you that I love *you*. That it's over between us. That . . ." He can't finish his sentence, then clumsily wipes the tears out of his eyes, and that makes me cry, too. I cry for

Chance and me, and for Lucille because she didn't get any of the money she deserved and because my name had been my father's last word. I cry because my father is dead. Finally. I cry until it hurts.

"I don't know what to say," Chance says, and I burst out laughing because he never knows what to say when confronted with my feelings. He looks at me as if I've lost my mind. Maybe I have.

Ben would know what to say, I am sure of that. He would have pulled off the road right then and there, cuddled me like I was a kid. He has been wounded, too, and only those who hurt know how to give comfort.

"Hil probably figured he'd taken care of her for all these years. Probably figured you and Rose would look out for her, which I know you will. Hil had his own way of figuring out things. That's the way your father was. He could be selfish like that. But he took care of what was important to him. You and Rose. You've got to give him that."

It has rained all week, been sunny most of the day, but now a lazy, misty rain has come back, leaving lacy patterns on the windshield. Chance turns to an all-news station, and the staccato voice of the announcer increases the tension in the car. I roll down my window and let the rain hit my face.

"We're going to have to buy a new car. We're not going to be able to get another lease. Every month some shit comes up, and we're late with payments." Chance slides effortlessly from my father and the past into money and the future. We have two cars, both leased. A small BMW and a large Explorer, which is ridiculous for just the three of us. "As soon as the estate is settled, we'll be able to—"

"He died just in time to take care of our debts, right?"

"You know I'm not saying that, Dani, how could you think I would say something like that?"

"Well, that's exactly what you said. As soon as the estate is settled." I'm baiting him because I'm mad and want him to be angry, too.

"That money belongs to you and not to us. It's yours."

"We spend too much damn money." I offer a veiled apology for my bitchiness.

"*You* spend too much damn money." He throws it back in my face.

"Fuck you!"

He snaps off the radio, so there is just the rain and the drone of the engine.

We turn into our driveway, which circles the front of our house and makes it look grander than it is. I jump out of the car, slam the door behind me, and run down the pebble walk to our two-story house.

We've lived here for five years. We bought it when Teddy was two because we wanted him to have a backyard, which he has now, and to grow up around kids from similar backgrounds. We wanted him to have a "neighborhood," live a "normal" childhood, which neither of us had, and this place offered it. Everything came with it—the kitchen appliances, flower bed in the backyard, weedless lawn like a carpet, ready-made neighbors.

All of the houses resemble one another, although they vary in size and structure. They're all made from the same brown brick and stucco; all have fireplaces, decks with barbecue pits, high ceilings, parquet floors, three bathrooms. They're designed to look like the kind of house I grew up in but unburdened by age. The toilets flush without problems, the lights shine bright, there are no dead electrical sockets or windows you can't close. They're like houses on a movie set, cardboard fronts that look authentic.

Our neighbors—the Browns, Irwins, Carmichaels, Winstons—could be actors on the same set, young black professionals playing interchangeable roles. We all spend too much money and pretend to be ashamed of it. We all went to college around the same time, one or two went Ivy League, several to Spelman and Howard, others to state universities. The men have "good" jobs and make "good" money. Nobody has ever been laid off, arrested for a crime, or done shameful things. Chance and I have a certain status because of my father. Nobody knows about my mother.

We protect and assure each other of our worth and status. We make play dates for our children. They attend the same birthday and Halloween parties in the same neat, clean backyards. We are "friends" and know as much of one another's business as it is safe to know. I wonder how they would feel about me if they knew about Ben.

He has been calling me for two days because he wants to know what has happened. I was supposed to leave Chance on Wednesday, the day my father died. Ben had given me an ultimatum. I haven't returned his calls.

Two months ago, Ben gave me a choice. We were in the bed he once shared with his late wife, Janey, sipping the chamomile tea he brews after we make love. When he kissed me, I tasted flowers on his lips. It was a tender kiss that said good-bye.

Ben is thirty-five, stocky, and built like a prize-fighter. If you saw him on the street, you wouldn't believe how tender he can be, how gently he holds me. He has the stance of a tough guy; I can walk into the roughest bar in the wildest neighborhood with him and feel safe. He has that take-no-shit attitude that other men respect, although he'd rather talk his way out of a fight than use his hands, which are precious because he's a musician.

His bass is his passion. He plays jazz at various out-of-the-way clubs nobody has ever heard of with a trio of odd-looking men who love music more than money and are as close as brothers. When I'm with him, I'm somebody else, certainly not a wife-mother-daughter-sister, but a wild, mysterious woman, unpredictable and intriguing like the places he takes me. The first time I heard him play, I couldn't believe he could coax such sweet tones from so awkward an instrument. His fingers coax pleasure from my body as easily as they play.

When he's not playing bass, he works in the greenhouse he owned with his late wife. He hired somebody to manage it when she died, but he likes to be there because it brings her close. He doesn't talk much about his family, but his eyes will suddenly water without explanation and he'll drop his gaze, so I know they've come into his mind.

I met him at his greenhouse a year and a half ago. It was the third anniversary of the deaths of his wife and daughter. I was buying a plant for Randa, my next-door neighbor. I was standing at the counter holding a Swedish ivy, poised to ask the price, and out of the blue he told me that his wife, Janey, and his daughter, Bennie, had been killed three years ago that afternoon. They were hit by a truck as they were crossing the street in front of his home, he said. The driver was drunk, and had been convicted of vehicular manslaughter, but that didn't matter because they were gone.

I'd never seen such grief on a person's face. He explained that in that moment when he spoke to me, he'd had to talk to someone or go crazy. He apologized for "inflicting me with his anguish." I felt so sorry for him, I tried to think of something to say but couldn't. So I put my plant down and listened as he told me exactly what had happened that day. The last words he said to his wife. The way his daughter felt when he hugged her that morning.

"You remind me of somebody I once knew that I loved very much," I told him after a while, then realized it was a dumb thing to say because I didn't know him at all, but it was his despair that made me say it. I realized later that the person was my mother before she left me.

"That person is gone, too?" he asked, and I nodded.

We began to talk about other things then: the plants, the weather, the store. We talked for the next hour, went to get some coffee, talked some more. We never stopped.

"I can't take this anymore, Dani," he said the

day of his ultimatum. "I've been through too much already."

"What do you mean?" I asked, although I knew. He hesitated before he answered.

"You're keeping me dangling while you make up your mind about Chance, and I can't let you do that to me. You don't trust me enough to leave him, and don't trust him enough to leave me. You're caught between us. It's going to mess up everyone."

He was right. I am a selfish bitch, and I know it.

"But I love you," I said.

"You've got to make a choice, Dani, and once you've made it you have to stick with it. No matter what." He got out of bed, slipped on his underwear, and sat next to me on the edge of the bed. "The truth is, I should have known better. Women never leave their husbands for their lovers," he added with a sad little laugh.

"Sometimes they do."

"Usually with disastrous consequences."

I had told him about Mariah. I wished I hadn't.

"But I love you," I told him again.

"Then it's time for you to choose," he said.

So I did, and it was him.

That was two months ago. I started my own bank account, depositing measly adjunct professor's checks from my job, where I teach glorious moments of African-American history to college kids who couldn't care less. I secretly packed away all the things that matter to me—the jewelry Teddy made me in camp last summer, the journals I've kept since I was a kid, her brooch. I packed my sexy nightgowns and took them to Ben's, and told him I would tell Chance the following Wednesday. It was an arbitrary day; I'm not sure why I chose it.

Maybe leaving my marriage was simple daydreaming, lies that I told myself because my unhappiness seemed beyond toleration, because I left out the most important number in the equation—the essential person in my life. I hadn't considered what I would tell my son, Teddy. I never came up with the words I'd say or where he'd end up or how he'd feel, which was crazy considering what Mariah did to me, those useless words she'd uttered.

As it ended it up, it didn't matter.

They say that sick people can choose the moment when they die. They'll stick around until some beloved brother flies in from Mississippi or a favorite child leaves or enters a room, *then* they'll close their eyes and depart. I suspect that's what my father did, sensing at three o'clock on a Wednesday morning that his youngest daughter was up to no good, and so he took his step into eternity in time to keep her from messing up her life and her son's like his wife had done before her. He took his turn for the worst; Aunt Lucille called Rose and she called me, which is how I ended up sitting beside him in time to hear him say my name. If that was my father's goal, he sure as hell achieved it. Hilton Dells was one for that.

Maybe he was right.

If my life were a romance novel, one in which the unhappy heroine leaves her dull spouse for another man, Chance would be the lover. His name is perfect. It hints of wild, tender love and afternoons of reckless passion. It's a name that a woman who hasn't had more experience with authentic emotions and is prone to bouts of fantasy could easily fall in love with.

My mother was that kind of woman.

Chance has a black man's classic beauty. Skin the color of imported wood, a football player's shoulders and chest, perfect teeth revealing a smile that women believe was created just for them. I fell under its spell when I met him; we fell under each other's spell.

He rarely smiled then, which I found interesting because every man I knew smiled too much. I didn't realize until I married him how much of my father was in him, or maybe my father's presence in our lives stirred it to the top. Maybe that was half the attraction.

What I did realize was how much we had in common. For one thing there were our backgrounds, abandoned by unworthy parents, over-protected by older siblings, never sure exactly where in life we fit. There was also the rampant materialism that marks our generation. Designer this and name-brand that. BMWs when Hondas make more sense. Veuve Clicquot when Korbel's will do. Driving fast on dangerous curves, spending more money than we make, smoking weed at night, doing Ecstasy when we could find it, although we've stopped that now because of Teddy.

If I had to choose a color for my marriage it would be taupe—a nondescript shade between brown and gray. Good for a suit if you add a spot of red, lousy for a relationship. Our son Teddy is my spot of red.

Maybe moleskin is what marriage becomes when real life steps in. Maybe there's no such a thing as a "happy" marriage. Certainly the joke my parents had was a disaster for everyone involved, and cost one poor soul his life. It's hard to explain to a third party—even someone as empathetic as Ben—what exists between married people—the stories within stories, the fables about your relationship that you know by heart and believe. Every argument is the prologue to the next. After ten years, our marriage is a ball of yarn that won't unravel neatly.

We have no core. Sex, when we bother to have

it, is humdrum, boring to be exact. We talk about the *business* of being married—mortgage and car payments, money we owe, whose turn it is to feed the cat, who forgot to turn off the TV, whose fault it is our checks bounce. Our fights go on for hours, days. We start, then forget, then start again.

The man you fall in love with at twenty is not necessarily the one you love at thirty. If I met Chance today, I'm not sure if I would love him. Yet there are times when I know I would, when I forget the tension between us, when I put Ben out of my mind. That's when I pretend the missteps we take don't matter. I fall in love with Chance again. But then something happens. I'll recall some thoughtless thing he said that morning at breakfast and won't let myself forgive him; then each word is a recrimination. I think of Ben, fantasize about the last time we were together. I wonder sometimes if Chance knows about Ben and if he simply doesn't care. I wonder if he is still involved with Theresa Arcadia.

She is a twenty-six-year-old Italian girl who works for my father's company. She can pass for black if you don't look hard. Her long black hair falls in her face, and she's built like a black woman—big ass, voluptuous body, which will go to fat in five years if she's not careful. She smiles too much, and carries herself with a slutty strut that most girls drop in high school. She's smart, tough, and as ruthless as my father was, too brazen to be discreet.

Her calls to my husband always came in the name of business, and I believed him when he swore there was nothing between them. But then there were those looks exchanged discreetly at company functions, those silences that followed my entrance into rooms, those cute notes slipped into his briefcase. Then I caught them in a situation that was undeniable. My heart was broken. He wept, pleaded, swore their relationship was over, and I forgave him. But by then I'd gone to buy that plant for my neighbor Randa, and it was too late.

Or was it?

My cell phone, tucked in the bottom of my bag, rings again. I know it is Ben. I turn it off without answering it.

"Dani!" Randa of plant fame calls out from her front door as I open mine. She is plump and plain, with long beautiful hair worn straight down her back. She's proud of her hair and constantly curls it around her fingers or waves it out of her face. She thinks her hair is her best feature, but that's actually her smile, which is quick, slightly bucked, and makes you feel as if you've known her all her life. She once told me she overheard some drunk in her family say she was a "a waste of high yellah." She said it with a disdainful laugh, like it had hurt her then and it probably still did.

I don't like Randa's husband, Brent. He is as tall as Chance but big-boned, with flabby hands that grab and clutch. His clothes are custom-made, but he has a greasy style that makes a thousand-dollar suit look like he grabbed it off the rack in Wal-Mart. He makes more money than anybody else on our block, and Randa told me in secret he's been on her to move.

"Are you okay?" Randa's house shoes slap across the pebbles in her yard as she runs to greet me. "Chance called yesterday and told me what happened. Dani, I'm so sorry!"

"I'm fine." I return her hug.

"Where have you been?" she scolds me gently. "I've been calling your cell nearly every hour!"

So some of those calls I haven't answered must have been from Randa. "I haven't felt like talking to anybody," I say truthfully. "I've been spending a lot of time with my family. My sister and my aunt."

"Of course," she says and sighs. Randa is a woman of deep, understanding sighs.

"How are they doing?"

"Okay."

"And you?" Another sigh.

"Basically, I'm fine."

"Everyone was so upset to hear about your dad. I never met him but I heard so much about him. I think my dad met him once. He said he was a legend."

I was never sure what to say when people talked about the "legend" who was my father.

"Is it okay that I told everybody?"

"It doesn't matter if people know. It's in the paper today because the memorial service is tomorrow."

"Dani, when something happens like this you've got to open up to other people." Randa is a great believer in the healing properties of talking about your business. I don't share her belief. "Sarah and Charlotte are coming over later with some food. Is that okay? Come on, let's go in." She leads me into my living room not waiting for an answer. "Now you just sit down here and let me make you some tea."

The healing properties of tea, like those of talk, is another of Randa's beliefs. But I am thankful for her now. She hugs me again, swallowing me up in her ample bosom, the way Rose does, mothering me into submission. She goes into my kitchen, a carbon copy of her own. Randa is, of course, a perfect homemaker, spotless kitchen, cookies for kids when they come home from school, pizzas from scratch on Fridays. Teddy asked me once if he could live with her during the week and come home on weekends.

"How long have you had this honey, honey?" This is Randa's sorry attempt at wit as she peeks in from the kitchen holding a jar of honey filled with crystals. She comes in with a tray she's found somewhere in the mess of my kitchen, loaded with a teapot I didn't recognize that must have been hidden on a back shelf. She puts the tray down, clasps my hand again, and we sit there hand in hand like lovers or two lost girls.

I haven't had many friends in my life. In all my thirty years, I think there's been only one and that was Clarissa Elliot, Cassie, I called her, whom my aunt despised and I loved like a sister. She was a red-haired kid with a "bad girl" reputation, even though she came from a "good" family, as good as mine anyway. Her father was a doctor and her mother a drunk. Most of my black girlfriends didn't like her, but I had more in common with her than with them and what I saw as their perfect lives.

Cassie loved drama and dragged me along on her adventures. I smoked cigarettes with her for the first time, and we lost our virginity the same night, high on weed and rum, to two best friends—both black—in a seedy hotel near Newark Airport. We were freshmen in high school then, and it was the most daring thing we'd ever done. We both did drugs in high school. I tried coke, snorted heroin once, but it made me vomit so hard I never tried it again. I didn't like losing control, which was what Cassie was looking for. Our high school was full of druggies; everybody knew it but the parents. Cassie was heavy into coke, and fucked a big-time coke dealer for a while who tried to string her out. She claimed he had the biggest dick she'd ever seen, like fucking a maypole, she liked to say.

I don't know what she's doing now. She went to UC at Berkeley, dropped out her sophomore year, and never went back. I went to Hampton, my father's alma mater, then finished at Rutgers because I got sick of the fact that everybody knew him because he'd given so much money.

I missed Cassie more than I missed anybody in my life, except Mariah when she left. I invited her to my wedding, but she didn't show, and when I saw her again race and distance had put boundaries between us. I was pregnant with Teddy, intent upon putting my past, including my wild white girlfriend, behind me. Since the past was all we had, we didn't have much to say. It was a sad little meeting. We both hoped it would be more. We promised to stay in touch but never did. I have no idea what she's doing now. I miss her. Another precious person come and gone.

Randa is the kind of girl Cassie and I laughed at in high school. Never tried drugs. Virgin when she married. Believed and obeyed her parents. Everything always turns out right for her. I often wonder what would happen if some unbearable sadness dropped into Randa's life. She would probably muddle through, handle it with prayer and her belief in the ultimate sweetness of life, tea, and talk.

"Things will be okay," Randa says, squeezing my hand.

"No, they won't."

"Yes, they will! You've got people who love you, a husband who adores you, a good life. Everything will be okay."

"You really believe that?"

She cocks her head to the side, playing the mother I never had. "I wish I knew what to say, Dani. I don't know how it feels to lose a parent, someone you loved as much as you did your father. Is your mother still alive? Will she be at the funeral? You never talk about her."

"No."

"No, she's not alive, or not coming to the funeral?"

"Neither. She's dead."

"Oh, Dani, I'm sorry. I knew they were divorced, but I didn't know you'd lost her, too. I shouldn't have brought it up."

"It's okay." I comfort her now.

"Did your mother die when you were a child?" I know she is thinking about herself and her kids, how they would fare if something happened to her, putting herself in my mother's shoes.

"In college. Listen, I'm going to add some sugar to my tea." I hint that this is not something I want to talk about, and when I come back into the room Randa tactfully changes the subject.

Her husband, Brent, follows Chance into the room. Chance avoids looking at me, but when he does his eyes are filled with tenderness and make me sorry about what happened in the car.

"Anyone want a drink?" he asks.

"Yeah, man, I'll take one. Got any scotch, and not that cheap stuff you usually drink?"

"How about you, baby?"

"We'll stick with tea," Randa answers for both of us.

The doorbell rings and my neighbors Sarah and Charlotte come in. Sarah, a few years younger than me, is model-thin, with keen Ethiopian features. Charlotte, whom her husband calls "Red," has an exotic look that I envied when we met and sometimes still do. Chance pushes drinks at them quickly—wine for Charlotte, rum and Coke for Sarah.

"Are you okay?" they ask in unison. "Can we get you anything, do anything for you?"

"No, I'm fine." They take me at my word and soon everybody is chatting about things that don't matter to me. I sink back into my spot on the couch, oblivious to everything, thinking about Ben and what I am going to do and say and my aunt Lucille and finally about my mother, Maria-then-Mariah, dead, who has swooped back into my mind with my father's words—like some creature from the living dead. I can't picture her now. I close my eyes and try to, how she looked and felt, the rose perfume she wore. I hear my father say my name, but it is Chance.

"Dani!"

I open my eyes as if waking from a dream. Everyone is standing around me, concerned looks on their faces.

"She's really tired." Chance excuses me like he would a kid who has been up too late. I yawn, nodding like a kid does.

I hear Teddy in the distance, running into the room in fast little steps, like a puppy. Everyone laughs when they see him. My son brings light and laughter wherever he goes, even to other children's parents.

"Hey, little man!" Chance picks him up. Teddy scrambles to get out of his arms and runs to me, and snuggles up like he did when he was a baby, molding his body into mine.

"Mommy?"

I hug him tight, and my heart feels at rest, as if it had been wandering and finally found a place to settle. Teddy brings me back to myself. I hold onto him for dear life.

"Are you sad because Granddaddy went to Heaven?"

"He was old and got very sick very quickly."

"Are you and Daddy old?"

That brings a collective laugh from the group, even me.

"We're not going anywhere," Chance says. "We'll be around until *you* get as old as Grandpa."

Everyone leaves shortly after that. Chance takes Teddy upstairs to give him his bath, and I go to our room and lay out what I will wear to the memorial service. Black silk suit, cream crepe de chine blouse, alligator pumps and bag. I look in my jewelry box for something appropriate, pearls of course, then notice her brooch, tucked as if it were hiding from me in the lining. I pick it up, and that day comes back. I will wear it, I decide, pinned next to my skin like a charm, but I'm not sure if it will be a good or bad one.

I go into Teddy's bathroom, sit on the commode, and watch Chance bathe him. Teddy climbs into his Spider-Man pajamas, and Chance and I sit on the edge of his bed as he says his prayers.

When we go into our room, we undress in si-

lence. I was usually asleep when he came from
the office at night and angry because I imagined
he had been with Theresa. After Ben, it didn't
matter so much, because I was lying, too.

But I'm not angry tonight, and when he pulls
me close, I want to feel him ease his body into
mine. We make love, gently and passionately, better than we have in months as if our grief is fore-
play and my father's death has set me free. We lie
there afterward, holding hands, until Teddy
screams out from one of his nightmares and, eyes
still closed, crawls into bed between us.

"I'm scared," he says in his sleep. Chance holds
us both in his arms.

"Sometimes we all are," he says to Teddy, and
then whispers over Teddy's head, "I love you,
Dani. Everything will be okay, I promise you. I
will make everything okay."

I whisper back that I love him, too. I feel safe
and relieved, as if some terrible ordeal has finally
passed.

Later that night, when we've put Teddy back in
his own bed and I know Chance is asleep, I go
downstairs to call Ben. I tell him that my father
has died, and everything has changed. I say I love
him, but I have my son to think of and that the
best thing for me to do is to stay in my marriage.
He says he isn't Durrell Alexander. I say I don't
care, I just need to work things out with Chance,

and I don't want to see him again. He doesn't say anything for a time and then says that I have been bad for him, and he is sorry that he'd met me, and I know he is right. He says please not to call him again, because I used him to bring life back into my marriage, used him until I didn't need him anymore, and I say maybe he is right about that, too.

I feel empty when I hang up, as if something vital has been pulled out of me, but I know I have done the right thing. I am not my mother's daughter. Hilton Dells has had the last word, as usual. Everything will be okay, like Chance said it would be.

And it is until the next day.

Rose

seven

𝒥 have always been a keeper of secrets, my own, my mother's, and those of other people. Three months ago, Chance told me about his affair with Theresa Arcadia. He had broken it off, but now he will be haunted by it for the rest of his life. Before he died, my father told me the rest of the story, and my heart aches for them all. There's not much I can do about it except be there for Dani when the whole truth comes out. There is no way Chance will be able to explain that kind of betrayal, even though the choice belonged to the woman, not him. I promised my father I would keep it to myself. I'm a woman who keeps her word.

I know Dani's secret, too, although it is not nearly as destructive as that of her husband. I don't know the name of this man Dani thinks she's in love with, but names aren't important. Feelings are, as long as you control them. I've been out-thinking my baby sister since she was in diapers, and there's very little about her I don't know, which is not to say that I approve of what's happening but rather that I won't say anything until she decides to tell me herself. Maybe he will be there for her if and when she decides to leave Chance.

I knew about Max, my Aunt Lucille's secret lover until he died six years ago, which sent her into a depression that nobody noticed but me; our family is not one to take note of other people's pain. I know that she still visits his grave in New York on the anniversary of his birthday and his death. I'm sure that he wanted to marry her. I suspect that he was the great love of her life, but she chose to stay with us. She knew that *two* "mothers" running off with lovers in one lifetime was too much for two young girls to deal with, so she made the sacrifice. My aunt is the most generous, loving woman I have ever known, yet she often tries hard to keep *that* a secret.

Marshall, *my* secret lover, has been married for twenty years. We've been together for six. Our connection demands boundaries. I never let it get out of hand. Sometimes I think I love him.

He talks about his wife, Roberta, but never in detail. I know that she is baby-doll pretty and vain about her looks. She loves clothes and wears them well. She's an accountant by profession, and he's proud of her business acumen. She doesn't like sex but is good at faking it; she had him fooled for years.

She has fooled the world about her mothering skills as well. She appears to be a generous, warm-hearted woman who always puts her family first, but in reality she tears her children down with snide remarks and impossible demands. Marshall spends much of his time repairing the damage she subtly inflicts. My greatest fear is that she has guessed about me and is taking her revenge out on her family. I feel guilty when I think about that and ashamed that I have played a role in her un-happiness. But I need him, too. I want to believe that I offer him the support he needs to manage his marriage—for the sake of the children. They are all that matter.

I love his children. The middle one, the girl, is his favorite, although he'll never admit it. The youngest is most like him, but he doesn't see it. His oldest son occasionally disappoints him. I've bonded with his children through his stories about them. I know their habits and favorite TV shows. I know what frightens them, their favorite meals at McDonald's, what they do on weekends. I've seen them grow up through their photographs.

I'll never meet them. They're like the children

in my school. They come into my life, I love them while they're there, then let them go to live the lives they'll lead. I pray for them when they cross my mind.

Marshall shares only those parts of his life that fit into a Friday afternoon. I never ask for more. I am grateful for what he gives me, grateful that I can give myself as freely as I do. I was celibate for fifteen years before I met him. Until I slept with him, I had cut that part of my life away, ripped it out completely. Never masturbated, didn't own a vibrator. I forced myself to be dead inside.

I share my body eagerly and freely now, but none of my emotional life. I don't want our time together to be marred by sorrow. Mostly we talk about our schools. (He's a high school principal in the same city as me.) He knows who my favorite students are, and when they enter his realm he watches them like a guardian angel. We share their victories and defeats, toast them when they go to college, worry if they get into trouble.

Our lives intertwine only in these ways.

I keep my tender parts to myself.

I've learned my mother's lesson well.

I've never been one to tell all, especially when it involves an intimate part of my body as does this thing that I recently learned. Three weeks ago, I discovered a lump in my right breast. It wasn't there when I had my mammogram six months ago. I was in the shower, smoothing my puff filled with shower gel over my breast, taking in the scent of lavender gel, and there it was, nudging itself to my attention. I rinsed off quickly, toweled off, hoping it would go away, but, of course, it was still there. I dropped down on the seat of the toilet, my breath gone. I sat there for ten minutes then made myself get dressed for school, tried to forget about it. I would keep it to myself, I decided, like I do things that hurt me.

But I did call my doctor from work that morning and made an appointment for another mammogram. She has called me three times since then. I haven't returned her calls. I'm afraid of what she will tell me. I don't want to hear her words. I want to stay in this space of not knowing as long as I can. Each day in the shower I feel it, touching around it, making out the shape of it, the way it has pushed itself into my flesh, taking up space that doesn't belong to it.

I'm an intelligent woman, although my response to what has happened may not sound very smart. I need to keep this tucked inside me, as if exposing it to air might make it grow. I know the danger. I touch it at night before I go to sleep, then forget about it. My workdays are extremely busy, and it's easy to get lost in them. I go through them with no thoughts of myself, which is why I'm as good as I am.

The one person I share things with died two days ago. I meant the words I whispered to him, that I loved him, even though Dani couldn't believe that I did. My baby sister has never understood what was between my father and me. It saddens me that she, like most people, had so little understanding of him. I could tell him things I would never share with another living soul because we had the same inner core, the place where he hid things that nobody else could see. I was the only person he let in to see them. Maybe because I looked like him, and every time he looked at me he saw himself. Maybe because nobody else cared to know.

I will miss him.

With the exception of Aunt Lucille, I am the only person who will.

The sorrow he held within him had no end. He didn't allow himself to show what he felt, but that didn't mean he didn't feel it. I knew that much about him. We were alike in that, made of the same material.

"Pop." That was what I called him. "Pop" or "Hilton Dells," which I only said when we were alone; usually it was "Pop," which brought a scowl the first time I said it, and then a surprised smirk. I was fourteen then, too old for "Daddy," too young for "Father." "Pop" was so unlike him it suited him well.

"Pop, can we talk a minute?" I said to him shortly after I'd been to the doctor, the week before he died. He was in his study relaxing on his couch near the window, his feet in his worn leather house shoes propped up on the worn leather ottoman that he loved. He was reading the newspaper and glanced up at me with an amused expression that could also pass for annoyance, but I always saw through it to what lay beneath. I knew to put a time limit on our conversations. Too much talk made him uncomfortable, so we communicated on his terms. I accepted that about him.

He laid down his newspaper. I noticed how tired he looked.

"I found a lump in my breast."

He studied my face before he spoke. "What kind of lump?"

"What kind do you think?"

"What did the doctor say?" He picked up the newspaper, his eyes fastening on it, but I knew he wasn't reading.

"I don't know yet."

"What the hell do you mean you don't know yet? What did the tests say?" He glared at me, then dropped his eyes back to the newspaper. "Your grandmother died of breast cancer. She was stubborn, like you. Wouldn't go to the doctor and when she did she wouldn't let them take her breast, said what the Lord gave her no white man was going to take away. She was a limited, ignorant woman. So she died with it. Don't be afraid to face things. Rose. Don't be a coward like she was. Afraid of her own shadow."

"Coward" was the worst thing he could call somebody. I flinched when he said it. "Do you want to die, Rose?" There was such sorrow in his eyes.

"What the hell kind of question is that?"

"The kind that needs an answer."

"No, of course not!"

"So you've been to the doctor?"

"Yes."

"They've done some tests?"

"Yes."

"But they haven't gotten back to you with the test results, is that it?"

"I haven't returned her calls. I don't want to know yet."

"Why not?"

"I'm not ready yet."

"What does Lucille say?"

"I haven't told her. I will when I get ready."

"When will you be ready?"

"When I find out what the doctor says."

"That's crazy!"

"I know." I shrugged and rolled my eyes. He rolled his back.

"You are my daughter, aren't you. Stubborn and foolish."

"Stubborn, not foolish."

"And Dani? What does she say?" The mere mention of Dani's name made him smile, but he never let her see it. I often wondered why. It amazed me that she couldn't see how much he loved her.

"I haven't told Lucille, I haven't told Dani."

"Come on, MissLady." He used the pet name he hadn't used in years and beckoned me to sit beside him. I squeezed down next to him on the couch. He gave me an awkward, self-conscious hug. His obvious discomfort amused me, and I hugged him back.

"You'll be okay, MissLady."

"I'm not so sure."

"You'll be okay, because you're tough like your old man. It will take more than this to take you out. You got too much of me in you."

"And not enough of the other?" I watched his face as I always did when I mentioned my mother, but it was inscrutable.

"Not enough of the other," he said finally, giving me that. He unfolded the newspaper again, hinting that this moment of parental intimacy was up. I moved to the chair next to him. Neither of us spoke. I was used to these silences; they said more than our words.

"Did Chance tell you about Theresa Arcadia?" He kept his eyes on his newspaper, which told me that this particular piece of information was painful.

"He told me he had ended their relationship, but I advised him to tell Dani, and he did."

"Not that. More than that. She's pregnant, that Arcadia woman. Won't get rid of it. I thought the girl had more sense, but she's trying to play us all for what she can get. If I'd known that was what she was, I'd have fired her when I first found out about the two of them."

"You should have. It hurt Dani that you didn't."

"Don't you think I thought about that? If I had, she would have sued the firm for sexual harassment, and with good reason. I knew that much about her. I'm surprised Chance couldn't see how vulnerable he made us. Anyway, I plan to fire her next month. To hell with the consequences. It's an impossible situation. I've got a mind to fire his black ass, too," he added, his shoulders tightening. His eyes met mine. "Take care of Dani when she finds out. Be there for her. But don't say anything yet. Maybe I can figure a way out of this mess without the firm ending up in court and my family dancing to that woman's tune."

"I won't say anything."

He smiled, then added sadly, "She was the one who was most wounded by us, wasn't she.

Dani." My mother and he were the "us" he was referring to.

No, Pop, it was me, I thought, but couldn't share that truth with him at this late date. He folded his paper in half and leaned back, his eyes as sad as I've ever seen them. I wonder now if he had a premonition of what would come.

Two days later he had the stroke, and except for those few obscure words he muttered to Dani about opening a door, it was the last time he spoke. Chance's secret about Theresa's pregnancy weighed nearly as heavily on my mind as my own.

It is Friday. At last. The day I visit Marshall in "our room." I am running late because of the meeting with my family, and afraid I will miss him. My heart is pounding as I drive down the Parkway and off the exit. I need to be with him. I haven't told him about Dani and Chance, and I certainly haven't told him about the lump. He didn't bargain for that part of me.

Our room, which is jointly paid for, is a furnished one with an adjoining bath, which takes up the third floor of a splendid old Victorian located in a run-down neighborhood. The owner, a woman named Margaret who goes by "Pol," is a large, pleasant person with unbecoming orange hair worn in an untidy bun. She has a boisterous laugh that matches her frame and pours out of her in gales of merriment when you least expect it. I told her I was renting the room as a private getaway, an office away from noisy kids and prying family members. She gave me a sympathetic smile, but I'm sure by now she knows what we use the room for. We always pay six months in advance, a promise to ourselves that our relationship will last at least that long. We're her oldest tenants.

Our room has three small-paned windows that look out into the backyard, a marble fireplace that works, a comfortable king-size bed, and an old-fashioned Mission rocker. We've added personal touches over the years: a small refrigerator to store champagne and cheese, ridiculously expensive sheets of Egyptian cotton I send out to be laundered every week, vases of various sizes and colors for the flowers Marshall always brings. I imagine I can smell their fragrance on my clothes long after we leave.

We don't look like secret lovers, but rather two middle-age educators who might meet for lunch or tea at a respectable hour in a reasonably priced restaurant, the kind of responsible adults who pull out photographs of their children and always try to pick up the check. We're both slightly overweight, me more than he. He likes plump women; his wife is very thin. I could tell by the way he first touched me all those years ago that he loved what I euphemistically call my overripe body, which I've always been ashamed of. It was easy to take my clothes off that first time. I hadn't been naked in front of a man in more than a decade. His kindness made it easy. He's not a dazzlingly handsome man but very good-looking. His smile is quick and tender; his eyes betray what he thinks. They say that I am beautiful, and that he will never hurt me and that I am safe with him.

Our lovemaking has become more tender than passionate. At first there was the excitement of discovery, of remembering what I'd let die. He gave that back to me, and I'm comfortable with sexual feelings now. I never thought I would be again.

He is arranging tulips when I come into the room.

"My father died Wednesday. The memorial is tomorrow." I say it casually, deliberately so.

He puts down the flowers, takes me in his arms, hugs me and tenderly kisses my forehead. "I read it this morning in the paper, Rose, why didn't you call me?"

I shrug. The truth is, that was out of the question. We never call each other during the week. He hadn't called me when he got his promotion or when his house caught fire or when they found that his daughter was diabetic.

"Are you okay?" He searches my face for feelings I am trying to hide. I'm good at that, and he knows it.

"It's going to take awhile. I just know that I'll miss him in ways that I'm not even aware of yet. We were close, but—"

"Not that close?"

"No. Actually, we were closer than I am to most people."

"So you kept your distance from your father, too?" There is amusement in his voice, but it isn't cruel.

"I talked to him more than I did to anybody else. Almost as much as I talk to you."

We undress without speaking, get into bed. I snuggle close to him, and he holds me, touching my shoulder with his lips, then kissing the nape of my neck at the spot where hair meets skin. We lie there, we do that sometimes, me feeling the rhythm of his breath, like a baby tucked underneath her mother's heart.

"You feel like talking?"

"About what?"

"About what you feel, Rose. Or don't want to feel. About your father and what he meant to you."

"You sound like a shrink."

"I've honed my craft well on withdrawn, hostile sixteen-year-olds. I'm sure I can handle a forty-something."

"Withdrawn and hostile?"

"Never hostile."

I shift my body from his. He catches me and pulls me close to him. I can feel him getting hard against the tender part of my stomach. He eases away, not ready to make love.

"I ever tell you I played quarterback in college?"

"Where did that come from?"

"Filling the uncomfortable silence."

"I know another way to fill it." I touch the hollow of his chin with my tongue and then run it down the length of his body, burying my face in the hair at the bottom of his stomach, easing my tongue down the length of his penis and back again, then slowly come back up.

He shakes his head, and kisses me. "You're avoiding what's important."

"You don't think this is important?"

He laughs and shakes his head again. "You know better than that!"

"So you think whether you've told me you played football in college, is more important than having sex? Yes. Half a dozen times you've told me. Since when am I so withdrawn?"

He gives me the serious look, the one I'm sure he bestows on his reluctant sixteen-year-olds. "Not socially, emotionally. You know that as well as me."

I drop my eyes from his gaze the way his teenage students probably do and sit up. "My father and I had a complicated relationship," I say, letting the sheet fall from my breasts. "I loved him very much. Certainly more than many others did."

"Like Dani?"

I nod. "Their relationship was bad because of things that happened when I was a kid, I, well— you know how that goes with parents."

"No, tell me."

"You're playing shrink again." Like a therapist, he sits there with no expression on his face, waiting for my answer. "Can we just make love?" I beg him, sounding like a spoiled kid.

"No. I want to talk for a while."

"About what?"

Serious eyes again. "You've just lost your father, Rose. You're acting as if it's no big thing, and I know how deeply you feel things because of the kind of woman you are. Something's not adding up."

He slips on his shorts, his erection gone, then plugs in the electric kettle, and we wait for its whistle. I put on my robe. There is distance between us now, and there rarely is. When the water boils, he goes to the chest of drawers and takes out three bags of ginger tea, places them and the water into a red teapot, lets it steep for a moment, then pours it into mugs. The ginger is strong, and tickles my throat when I sip it.

"You're a mystery to me," he says.

"I'm a mystery to myself."

"You try to be everybody's strength. Whenever your name comes up, people say how great you are. How strong. How perfect, I hear that a lot. Teachers, kids, parents. Dr. Dell? Rose Dell? She's really great!"

I acknowledge what he's said with a reluctant nod, and he continues. "There's more to you, but I'm afraid if I touch it, try to penetrate it, things between us will end."

I shrug because I know he is right.

"You protect yourself in ways you're not aware of. I don't know how I feel about this arrangement we have. Sometimes I think I'd leave my wife in a New York minute for you—"

"Don't say that!"

"Other times, I know it wouldn't work between us, that all we'll ever have is these four walls, which is the way you want it."

"I am who I am." I turn into one of my sullen first-graders. "You sound like you're about ready to walk out that door and not come back." My voice is cool but my heart is pounding. I want to beg him not to say any more, to let things be as they were. But something in me won't let the words come out.

"Sometimes I know I'm in love with you," he says after a minute. "And then I think how much more of you I need, how much more I want."

"I can't give any more." My eyes fill with tears. They begin to run down my face; I can't stop them.

"I know that, too," he says. "Rose, I've told you practically everything about me there is to tell. You know about my wife and kids, what happens at work, my favorite color. You know how much I weigh and how every damn diet I go on fails because I love ice cream and bread. You know my mother's name and where she was born and my weakness for ginger tea.

"I know nothing about you. If you were to drop out of my life this afternoon, I wouldn't know what flowers to buy to remember you."

"Roses, of course," I say, then add quickly, "lilacs. They're my favorite. I love flowers with a fragrance."

Worried, he glances at the bouquet of tulips he'd brought me.

"And the ones kind men bring," I add. "The thought is more important than the smell."

"Your favorite color? What's that?"

"Rose, of course." He looks doubtful. "Turquoise."

"Your favorite TV show?'

"*The Newshour* on PBS." He rolls his eyes. "*General Hospital*. I tape it so I can catch up with what's happening while I eat my dinner. I've watched it since I was in high school."

"When did you start keeping secrets?"

"Secrets?" I joked, but he wasn't having it. "When I was seventeen."

"Why?"

"Because someone's life depended on it."

"Whose life?"

"Mine."

"What do you mean?"

"Because once you keep a big secret, it's easy to not tell small ones"; I avoid what I know he wants to find out.

"What was the big secret?" He won't let me hide.

"I'm not ready to tell it yet."

"You're hiding from yourself."

"No, just from other people."

"Two more things for now. Just two. Why was your relationship with your father so complicated?"

"Because of something bad that happened when I was a kid."

Apprehension shadows his eyes. "Did he molest you?"

"No, not that kind of bad," I quickly say. "Between him and my mother."

"What happened?"

"She left us. She ran off with her lover, then shot him to death a few months later." I go to the small table where the teapot sits and pour myself another cup, successfully avoiding his eyes.

"So she went to jail?"

"Isn't that where they usually put women who murder their lovers?"

"Depends upon the woman and the lover."

"Yes. That's where she ended up."

"Were you and Dani allowed to see her when she was in prison?"

"There was no way my father was going to let that happen, and I'm not sure she would have wanted it anyway."

He leans back on the bed, crosses his legs at his ankles. I settle next to him again. He drapes his arm around my shoulder, then lets it fall down my back, touching my hips, then folds his hands across his belly.

"In the five years we've been together, you've never mentioned her. What was her name?" he asks after a moment.

I don't answer because I'm not sure myself sometimes. "Maria, but she called herself Mariah." I take my cue from Aunt Lucille.

"She must be out of jail by now. Is she still alive?"

"As far as I know. I've tried very hard to put everything that happened back then out of my mind. I can't afford to think about it."

"You know from Psych one-oh-one that the only way to become an adult is to come to terms with and forgive your parents, no matter what they did."

"That's what they say."

"Will you tell me what happened in your family?"

I glance up, wondering if I want to go through the whole damn thing again, then his eyes, as they always do, pull a piece of it out of me.

eight

"MissLady" was my father's pet name for me, a not-so-subtle rebuff to his wife, hinting that I, his oldest daughter, was really the "lady" of his life. My father had a cruel streak in him nursed by frustration, racism, and plain, old-fashioned orneriness that touched everyone but me. I was his favorite. That brought me certain privileges. I was unshakeably loyal.

"What new life lesson has MissLady learned today?" he'd ask as he slammed the front door behind him, shutting out that part of his world. He never talked about that world, but I understand now how hard he worked to secure what he managed to create. He fought for everything he got against all the odds that then confronted ambitious black men. He did it because it was expected of him. People depended on him, his family as well as his workers. At times it must have seemed as if he carried a hundred people on his back.

He would toss his brown tweed coat across a chair in the living room, to be picked up by my mother or Jessie, her part-time helper. Jacket off, slippers on, anemic kiss planted on my mother's waiting cheek, he'd retire to his study and pour himself a drink, scotch, always the best. I'd greet him like an eager pup welcoming the master home.

If I was the "lady" of the household, then who was she? I was the buffer between them. I realize now that he subtly played us off against each other, and I came out on top. In some ways, he set us up for what happened later, yet I can't find it within me to blame him. I loved him too much for that.

My mother wasn't a full-grown woman when I was born, and it took turning twenty-one myself to fully realize just how young she was. Too damn young for a baby by a man who didn't know how to show his love. And my mother *needed* love more than any woman I've ever known. She soaked it up like a sponge does water, no matter how fetid it turned out to be.

There were twenty-one years between Maria and me, the same number as between her and my father. From an early age, it was clear to me who the adult was in their relationship—who made decisions, praised, scolded, disciplined. I was grown before I realized just how humiliating that must have been for her. She was more sister than mother to me, which was one reason I kept her secret—our secret—despite everything that happened. Sisters don't betray each other.

I see my mother when I look at Dani—her nose with its Ethiopian cast, rosebud lips girls now buy silicone to get, hair so thick and beautiful it can break a comb. Maria-who-called-herself-Mariah dipped in bittersweet chocolate, my Aunt Lucille once said about Dani. I always thought my mother was the most beautiful woman I'd ever seen.

That must have been what Durrell Alexander thought, too.

I knew she was up to something. I'd read enough romance novels to decipher the signs. I figured out what was happening probably before she did. He would call when she wasn't there. It got so I could recognize his voice. It was interesting. *Interesting*. A word I used when I didn't want to admit how affected or puzzled I was. His voice evoked a strange feeling in me that I wasn't prepared to face. It was a decidedly masculine voice, when the ones I knew were still cracking from adolescence and just beginning to deepen. It had an *interesting* rhythm to it. Hypnotic. We began our own sly flirtation.

I tried to imagine what he looked like. My fantasies swung between the exotic, daring looks of the two guys in *Miami Vice*—fast-talking, oozing sex, sleeves rolled up, and the smoothness of

Marvin Gaye. I would stand behind the kitchen door where she couldn't see me when she spoke to him, listening to every word she said. Teenagers routinely spy on their parents. If she had been older and smarter about kids and cheating, she would have realized that and been more discreet, but my mother was not one to hide her feelings, and she couldn't hide them from me.

I'm older now by two years than she was when she left us, and time has made me generous to us both. I understand the tension between mothers and their teenage daughters—the competitiveness edged with admiration, the unpredictable anger bound tight with stinging love. One becoming aware of her sexual desirability, the other sensing the loss of hers when she gazes at her daughter's firm, young flesh.

At sixteen, I knew far more about sex than my mother did. I'd lost my virginity at fifteen at a friend's sleepover. Her parents slipped out, and my boyfriend *literally* slipped in. Sex was an interesting study for me. At thirteen, I'd lifted a copy of *The Joy of Sex* from a neighborhood bookstore and, good student that I was, studied it like a manual, learning to explore parts of me that felt good to touch—my clit and nipples, the tight, soft walls of my vagina. I'd stroke myself to orgasm at least twice a week.

I suspect that my mother was a virgin when she married. She seemed to have grown up in a different era, before her time—circa 1930—in a pretentious, Nella Larsen world where tragic mulattoes reigned and men married for "good" breeding and "better" hair. My grandmother Mai must have been a piece of work. There's a photograph of her that I used to look at when I was a child. She had a tight, painful smile etched on her lips as if it were embarrassing to smile. I don't think I would have liked her.

I found my mother's ignorance about sex baffling and annoying. She was impressed but at the same time resentful of my knowledge, which I occasionally shared. She would watch me undress sometimes, her curious eyes fastening on every article of clothing I wore. I loved fancy, lacy underwear, which she noticed but never commented on. Sometimes I felt as if she were trying to steal some secret from me, take something I was unwilling to give. I don't think she was even aware of her feelings.

"Why do you try to act so old, Mom?" I would ask her.

"Because I *feel* old, Rosie," she would tell me. No one else called me Rosie. I loved to hear her say it.

I try to envision myself that year, to find the Rosie who became the Rose I am now. I was a "good girl" according to my teachers and friends' parents but had a mischievous, sneaky side I kept well hidden. I was an expert shoplifter, adept at swiping costly items from high-end stores. Bras and panties, always lacy, usually pink, were my favorite acquisitions. They called the cops on me once at Abraham and Straus, but the guard, who was black, knew my father, and I cried so hard he let me go. I tucked my hair up and went to Bloomingdale's the next week.

I was a disgusting snoop, seeking out my mother's secrets with stealth and determination. Hawklike, I watched her comings and goings, jotting down dates and times—when she left, when she returned, what she was wearing. Thursday—my father's late night—was her favorite day of escape. She would sneak in ten minutes before he came home, and if caught, claim she was visiting her best friend, Trish. I knew she was lying.

I routinely searched her drawers for evidence against her, even though in a corner of my heart I didn't want to believe what I suspected. I looked for photographs of them together, incriminating notes, anything that would condemn her. Once I found a photograph of my dead grandfather with her perched upon his shoulders. She looked like Dani at that age, same bright, eager eyes, funny little grin. I held it close to my heart, communing with this man—and this child—with whom I had no true connection. Another time, I found a letter from Trish written the month I was born.

I can clearly see why you love her so. I can only imagine how happy you are. Rose is the most beautiful baby I have ever seen. You finally have the happiness you have always deserved.

Ashamed, I put it back and slammed the drawer closed.

The next week, though, I found what I had been looking for, tucked deep within the folds of her lingerie. A note from him, vivid with descriptions of her body, what they did, how and where they did it. I threw the letter in the toilet in disgust. But his words excited me. Haunted me.

Two weeks later, I confronted her. I was sitting on my bed, supposedly studying for a chemistry test. It was my weakest subject, and if I wanted to keep doing my extracurricular activities, I had to maintain my GPA of 3.6. I was a superstudent, plastering over my feelings about what was happening in my family with good grades and super achievement.

A boy in my English Lit class had sent me an anonymous note teasing me about the size of my breasts—dumb teenage stuff. I was sure it was this varsity football player who sat two seats down from me, but I wanted proof. I'd secretly torn a page out of his notebook that afternoon and was comparing the handwriting, a gotcha smile on my lips. When she entered Dani's room, I turned down my radio so I could hear what they were saying.

"Does He watch everybody all the time?" I heard Dani ask. She had a reedy little voice. Every now and then the voice of a child at school will have that same pitch and timbre and stop me short.

"Who, Dani?"

"God."

"Of course he does. He sees everything we do and hears everything we say. He knows when we're being good and bad."

Lying bitch, I thought, a smirk on my face. You lying bitch. That was a word I never said out loud, but I thought it often enough in those days. They throw that word around like it's nothing now, but it meant something back then. I felt both evil and virtuous when I called her that.

Was it carelessness or was she simply tired of hiding it?

Even now, I'm not sure.

"I love you, baby," she said to Dani, the innocent. "I love you and Rosie more than anybody in the world."

More than him, I said aloud but knew she couldn't hear me.

She turned off the light in Dani's room, came through our joint bathroom, and peeked into mine.

"Don't study too late, honey."

I slammed my chemistry book closed.

"What's wrong, Rosie?"

"Why did you lie to Dani?"

"Lie to Dani? What are you talking about?"

"Didn't you just tell her some shit about God watching everything you say and do?" I didn't usually curse around her, and "shit" made her cringe. She stepped into my room closing the door behind her.

"You may not think of God that way, Rose. But Dani's a little girl and—"

"So He sees everything, right?" I was baiting her, and she knew it. She shifted uneasily.

"Say it, Rose. Whatever is on your mind, go on and say it."

I smiled mysteriously, playing with her. A cat fiddling with a wounded mouse.

"So God sees what you do, too, right, Mom?"

She dropped her head, then faced me squarely.

"Yes, Rose. I suppose He does."

"So does He see you getting it on with that dude who's always calling here? God sees that, right? Does He see you reading his dirty letters to you? Does He see you and Durrell Alexander?" I stretched his name out, screaming by then. She flinched at each word.

"You spoke to him? Why didn't you tell me?" She wasn't upset enough to hide her curiosity, and that enraged me.

"Ask him!"

She couldn't look me in the eye. She changed the subject, becoming the wronged, outraged adult, yet denying nothing.

"So you were in my things? Rose, you know better than to go in my things! How could you do that to me, go through my drawers like that?" She was crying now. I felt like crying, too, because I didn't want to see her cry. I forgot about everything in that instant but the tears in her eyes.

"I'm sorry," I said because I was.

"I'm sorry, too, Rose. I'm so sorry." She was asking me to forgive her. I remembered my anger and turned away. "Don't do that again, Rose. Promise me, you won't go into my things. There are private things that belong to me. I have a right to my own things." She sat down next to me.

I pulled away. "Things from him?"

"Who?"

"You know damned well who!"

She stood up, walked to the other side of the room. Looked out the window. I could hear Dani tossing in her bed in the adjoining room. I was grateful she was asleep. My father came into the house. I heard him slam the door.

"Maria?" he called out.

"Up here, Hilton. I'm up here with Rose. He's a friend of Trish's," she whispered, her voice desperate. "Those letters were what he sent to Trish."

"Then why do you have them?"

"She gave them to me."

"Does my father know him?" She turned then and faced me, woman to woman, her eyes admitting the truth.

"You know the answer to that, Rosie," she said.

"You really are a liar," I said. "I hate you!"

"What did you say?" Her voice was soft, timid.

"I said you're a liar and I hate you!"

"Sometimes I hate me, too," she said. The way she spoke, with such sorrow and self-doubt crushed the anger from me.

She sat down on my bed and wept with her head in her hands like Dani did, and I put my arm around her as she sank her head into her chest. I was her sister now, and nothing else mattered. I took her hand in mine, then played with her diamond ring, the one that belonged to my grandmother, like I used to do when I was a kid. She kissed me on the forehead. I laid down on my bed. She pulled the cover to my chin. I closed my eyes. She kissed my eyelids.

"Good night, my Rosie," she said.

For the next two weeks, we went back to the way we were. I went to school the next morning, aced my chemistry test, confronted the jock about his nasty note, went to my activities—Spanish Club, Debate Club, Pep Squad—as if nothing had happened between us. Six weeks later she was gone. But I knew where to find her. She had written her address for Dani, and two weeks after she left, I looked for her.

I told my aunt I had band practice that day, then took the bus to Port Authority. I asked somebody how to get to 110th Street and rode the Number 2 subway uptown. I found the building, counted up to their floor so I could watch the lights in the window, and stood outside hoping she would come out. I finally got tired of waiting and went back home. Four days later I was back, waited for an hour, went home, then came again the next week. This time I saw her as they were leaving the building. She was walking with him, hand in hand, dressed in wide flowing pants and a madras blouse that crossed at her breasts. Her hair flew loose around her face; it had grown back by then. I stepped back where they couldn't see me. She glanced behind her, as if she could sense my presence, and I saw her face, her gypsy earrings bouncing as she turned her head. I put my hand over my mouth so I wouldn't call her name.

He was taller, thinner than I thought he would be and moved like a dancer, smooth and cat-graceful. After she'd turned back around, he glanced back, too. I stepped out of the shadows then, straight into his view. He looked at me hard, familiar, and I knew in that instant that this was the way he looked at her, and it pricked something quick and warm in the pit of my stomach.

I came back the next day at the same time, followed them into the subway station, stood in the darkness until the train came. I boarded the car behind theirs, stood between cars watching them, got off when they did. I followed them for half a block until they came to a small off-Broadway theater. He went in first, but before she did, she stopped, threw back her head, and began to laugh, recklessly, as if this were the happiest day of her life. Her laughter tinkled like breaking glass and tore deep into my heart.

So that was what I did for the next few months. Stalked my mother and her lover. Until it was over.

"When was the last time you saw her?" Marshall asks me.

"Before she killed him." This was the first time I'd told this much of it to anyone.

"And you haven't seen her since?'

"No."

He pours some wine, cuts a chunk of Roquefort, places cheese and crackers on a glass platter, brings them into our bed. I gobble the cheese and crackers like a kid, finish off the wine in two gulps.

"Your father is dead, and despite what she's done, she is still your mother. Don't you think it's time you found her?"

In that place inside me where secrets dwell, I know he is right.

Saturday

Lucille

I didn't recognize her at first. I had seen her at the cemetery, a plain gray-haired woman who lingered near the edge of my parents' gravesite, close enough to observe yet not be seen by others. I assumed she was some mourner come to bid good-bye to a recently deceased loved one buried nearby. She wore a navy polyester suit trimmed with white buttons and piping. I could tell it was polyester by its cheap, gauzy sheen. It was a size too big for her.

She was thinner than I remembered. I'd once envied her voluptuous body as much as I had her pretty hair. My brother used to stroke that hair as if it were a living thing, but it was short now, cut in a dull, unremarkable style. Although we are the same age, she looked far older. Her life choices had cost her dearly; the price was written on her face and in the stoop of her body. I felt a pang of sorrow. Age has softened me.

Later, I see her at the memorial service we are holding for Hilton in his building. Fifteen rows of collapsible chairs have been set up in the lobby to accommodate those paying their respects. The room is filled with wicker baskets laden with roses, carnations, and irises. I've come early to search for papers Hilton mentioned before he went into his coma. The rest of the family hasn't yet arrived. Avoiding the elevator, I spot her as I head toward the stairs.

She is sitting in an aisle chair in the last row nearest to the door. Her hands are folded in her lap and her head is bowed. She sits stiffly, as if ready to bound out of the door at short notice. My heart begins to pound, and I step into a nearby stairwell, then risk another glimpse to be certain. It is her; I'm sure of it.

My first impulse is to alert Isaac, the security guard who has worked in the building since my brother bought it. He was the first man Hilton hired. He'd spent his youth in prison and was grateful to my brother for taking a chance on him. Next to Margaret Hanover, my brother's executive secretary, he was his most loyal employee. Should I ask Isaac to throw her out, I wonder? It had always been my duty to protect my nieces from her "corrupting presence," as my brother put it, but that responsibility died with him Wednesday morning. Truth was, I never agreed with most of it anyway.

His decision to keep them from her was a mistake. So many letters she sent them, all retrieved and thrown away. But they were *his* daughters. I was just the aunt, as he reminded me from time to time, so I never fought him on it. But he was wrong. A child needs her mother. There is no substitute. Life, though, always takes care of itself. Maria is alive; Hilton is dead. She will have the last word. Is she here to speak it?

I despised her once for her selfishness and the pain she caused my family. I've learned, though, to be less judgmental of others and of myself. I certainly benefited from her mistakes. Her girls are more mine now than hers. I took their rage at her and turned it into love for me. I no longer condemn her, this Maria who called herself Mariah.

"Are you all right, Miss Dells?" Isaac asks. My expression must have revealed my thoughts. He grabs my arm as if afraid I might faint. "May I take you to your seat?"

"I'm fine, Isaac." I shake off his hand, change the subject. "It's going to be a big crowd, isn't it?"

"Mr. Dells was a good man, Miss Dells. A good man. We're sure going to miss him around here. Young Mr. Carter has been doing a nice job though, he sure has, that young man. Mr. Dells taught him everything he know." His gaze drops from mine, afraid he has overstepped his boundaries. My smile reassures him that I appreciate his words.

"If you need anything, Miss Dells, you just let me know."

I assure him that I will, then quickly step back into the stairwell to watch Maria Dells.

Where is she living now? How far has she traveled to get here? She studies each woman's face as she passes, searching for features she hasn't seen in twenty years, wondering, I suppose, if her children will recognize her. If Dani sees her, I am certain that she will. Dani's face is her mother's.

After a while, she settles back in her seat and surveys the lobby. I am certain that the memories she has of Hilton's building are far different from mine.

This was and still is a grand old building. Hilton had done the most extensive renovations on an office building that folks around here had ever seen. The lobby is impressive, the wood paneling stripped and stained to its original luster, the parquet floors polished until they shone like glass. A Persian rug bought years ago at an auction in Manhattan covers nearly the whole lobby, and an antique chandelier hangs from the ceiling. It was the chandelier, glistening and whispering the power of white folks' money, that first drew my brother to this building. It sold cheap. The original owners were eager and determined to rid themselves of it and leave a community where black families had begun to settle. He paid half of what it was worth.

"Aunt Lucille, what on earth are you doing all the way back here?" Dani surprises me with a peck on my cheek. She has always been the most affectionate of the two, and the closest to me because she was so young when I came into her life. Rose is my brother's child in more ways than one.

"Sit with me, Grandma." Teddy grabs my hand, and I stoop to kiss him. As far as the world knows, I am his grandmother, and he has always called me that; no one has ever corrected him. I call him "Sweetums," which is what my mother called me. I glance over his head at Maria Dells. She seems oblivious to us and everyone in the room.

"I'll be there in a moment, Sweetums. I'm going to grab a smoke before I sit down," I say to Dani, who shakes her head in disgust, which makes me chuckle. "Please don't take over where your father left off. Where's Chance?"

"He said he had something to take care of before he came in. He's upset."

"He was very close to Hilton."

"No, it's something else." Dani is troubled, which concerns me.

"Don't worry, honey. We'll get through this together. Jamison will handle things. No one expects anything from us. I'll say a few words for the family, and that will be that. Your father wanted this short and sweet, and that is how it will be. He always said his legacy was his business, and it is."

"His business, not me and Rose?"

"Don't judge him harshly, Dani. You can't hold people accountable for who they are."

"Hey, you two!" says Rose joining us.

"Auntie Rose!" Teddy abandons my hand for his aunt's and hugs it against his cheek. He is an affectionate child, much as his mother used to be.

"Hey, honey. You and your mom go sit down and I'll join you in a minute. Where's your dad?"

Teddy points at the door, and Rose glances at it, then at Dani, suddenly concerned. She still protects her sister. In many ways, she is more Dani's mother even than me. "He'll be here, Teddy, don't worry. Are you doing okay, Aunt Lu?"

"I'm fine. Go on, you two. Take your seats. I'll be in shortly."

"She wants to smoke a cigarette," Dani says with an exaggerated eye roll.

"What's wrong, Aunt Lu?" Rose ignores her sister's comment. Foolish of me to think I can hide anything from this one.

"Nothing. It's just the day. The burial this

morning. What's to come. I'm as well as can be expected. Go sit down."

"Did you remember to give Lil a check for the
caterer?" Rose changes the subject. "Everything
has to be set up before we get back to the house.
They won't lift a finger unless they've been paid."

"Took care of it before I left. You two, go! I'll
come in with Chance."

Maria draws in her breath as the three of them
walk past then covers her mouth as if stifling a
cry. Her eyes follow them, hungrily taking them
in. Then she glances back, as if expecting someone to follow them. I step back. I don't want her to
see me. Some generous impulse tells me to let this
moment belong to her. But I can see tears running
down her cheeks.

Should I go to her, I wonder? Take her to the
girls, help them make peace with her at last? No.
She will find her own way to them, if it is to be
found. Perhaps all she wants is this moment. One
glance of the children she abandoned, maybe then
she will go back from where she has come. So
much time has passed. So much sorrow and too
many years. I suddenly feel nauseous. My
thoughts of the past, my lingering anger, and the
sweet, sickening smell of all those flowers over-
whelm me. I need air and a smoke to set me steady.
I step outside the building into the sunlight.

It is late afternoon, and the sun is fading but comfortably warm after the coolness of the lobby. I nod at several employees as they pass, then quickly light up a Winston, drawing the smoke in fast and exhaling with the pleasure I always feel with the first jolt of nicotine.

I never liked her. I am old enough now to acknowledge that fact and even the reason why I didn't. I considered her one of those pampered high-yeller girls who relied on their looks to get by. We were the same age but had nothing in common. As far as I could tell, she'd never cracked a book or newspaper, had no interest in anything to do with politics or black people, which was shameful considering the period in which we were young.

We were twenty when we met. I had graduated a year early from a black women's college in the South and was headed north to graduate school in New York City. She was my brother's wife, too eager to smile and please him.

College had been a wounding experience, which took me years to overcome. Southern black schools were rife with color coding and petty prejudices in those days, and a dark-skinned woman was the last thing one wanted to be. We were the last ones asked out or praised, never the campus queen or Greek "sweetheart." Dark-skinned men fared better—they were *men*, after all. They could choose their fate and usually chose women who did *not* look like their mothers.

So I made up for the way I looked by being smart, sophisticated, and ambitious. By the time I got to New York and the hip art scene of Greenwich Village, color didn't matter at all. I dated Jewish, East Indian, Asian, Swedish, British, French—anything but black men until I met and fell for Mel, who I loved until the day he died.

I was as prejudiced against women who looked like Maria as they were against women who looked like me. I was sure they despised us for reminding them of who they were. They often treated us far worse than some white women did—by simply not seeing or acknowledging us in social situations. By never giving us our due. Despite knowing better, a woman's color is still among the first things I notice about her—the shade of her skin, the texture of her hair, the shape of her nose. To this day, it riles me to be the only dark-skinned woman *not* carrying a tray in a party filled with affluent black couples. Old anger dies hard.

Much of what I felt about color I learned from my mother. Her skin was a deep, bittersweet chocolate. She never knew how beautiful she was. Annabel Dells was a "limited woman," as Hilton often put it. She was short and slight with hair that never grew no matter how many concoctions she put on it. "Tiny as a flea" was how she described herself. A *flea*, of all things. A nearly invisible, tiny black nuisance that stings and feeds off its host. It breaks my heart to realize how little she loved herself. Where did she learn such self-hatred? From her mother as well?

The guidance she gave me was always in the form of warnings: Never be "spoiled" by men, she would tell me. Never let a white man touch you. Stay away from jealous men and those without a job or money. Stay out of strong sunshine—don't want to get darker than you are. Never wear red—bring out too much grease in your skin. Don't wear white—make you look like a fly trapped in buttermilk.

These are the sayings I remember.

She owned very little, only a diamond ring that took my father five years to pay for, and which Hilton gave his wife when they married. I've never quite forgiven him for that even though she gave it back. I respected her for that.

My mother confined her life to the narrow place where she was born, the space where others insisted she belonged. She prided herself upon staying where she landed. Never been out of this town, she used to tell me, as if it were a virtue. What sad memories I have of that poor soul.

With nearly twenty years between us, Hilton and I grew up as only children. My mother married at sixteen, as they often did in those days, and was quickly pregnant with Hilton. My sudden appearance when she was thirty-six must have been an unwelcome surprise. I've always feared that it somehow contributed to her early death from cancer. She died when I was ten.

But my loss of her made me better understand the loss that my nieces must have felt. It helped me reach them in ways only I could, and I pride myself on what I taught them. They are bright, well-educated high achievers. They are women who could never live in narrow spaces, never refer to themselves as fleas.

I didn't know my father well. He worked as a carpenter for a rich white family who lived in a neighboring town. They were "good white folks," as the saying goes, who gave us their cast-off clothes, which my parents politely took but threw away, and books, which they taught us to treasure.

Hilton knew my father better than I and got his respect for education and hard work from him. Our father was dead by the time I was old enough to know him, and Hilton tried to be the father I never knew. He worked three jobs in college—as a short-order cook, a salesman, and a janitor in a building near the one he now owns. When he graduated he became a clerk in a white accounting firm that grew to admire his skills. When he began to make money on his own, he put me through college and lent me the money to buy the small apartment on Bleecker Street in Greenwich Village, where I met Mel on weekends and which I kept for years. I recently sold it for twenty times what I paid for it.

Although he could be selfish and hard, my brother built a charmed life of wealth, power, and respect. He was generous with his money and, despite my protestations, paid me well for caring for my nieces. I insisted that he take me out of his will; he'd given me enough already. With his guidance, I invested my earnings wisely. I will always be comfortable. These girls I raised are now strong women, and my responsibility to his family is over. Travel is my plan.

When I met my brother's wife, my first thought was that he had married a woman the color of that buttermilk where my mother had warned us flies never to play. His choice confirmed my opinion of black men, and her treatment of him confirmed my opinion of women who looked like her.

Now I understand that Maria Dells was as much a captive of other people's fears and fantasies as were Hilton and myself. Her "winning" color brought her nothing but shame. In my judgment of her, I was as limited as my own mother had been. It is a truth about myself that has taken me years to admit.

As I finish my cigarette and turn to go into the

building, I notice Chance standing in the parking lot, arguing with a young white woman. It seems a lively discussion. He gestures wildly, but the woman pointedly ignores him. She looks familiar, and I realize she is one of the firm's employees. After a moment or two, he leaves her standing by herself, rushing into the building with such haste he doesn't notice me waiting in the doorway until I grab his arm.

"What was that all about?" I am shocked by his expression. I take it for grief.

"Is Dani here?" He won't look me in the eye.

"What's wrong, Chance?" I have always loved this able young man who is so much like my brother.

"I have to talk to her."

"Can't it wait?"

"No, Lucille, it can't. I have to talk to her now. Before it's too late. I have to make her understand." His voice trembles, his eyes fill with tears.

Rose joins us then, and the look on her face tells me she understands what is going on. She glances at him and then at the woman as if disgusted by them both.

"Time you had that talk, isn't it?" she says to Chance. Irritation mingled with contempt is in her voice, which doesn't sound like her at all. "Past time you had it," she adds nastily as they walk into the building.

I'm not naive. The whole scene has the smell of some sordid sexual misadventure. But why today, why at my brother's funeral? My answer comes in the next moment when the woman, brazen as you please, comes toward the door. I know then what this is all about. So my dear Chance has done my brother one better. He's found himself a white woman, gotten himself the real thing. I step in her way, blocking her from entering my brother's building.

"You're Theresa Arcadia, aren't you?" I remember her name. I met her at company functions, and my brother had mentioned her more than once.

She seems surprised that I remember her. "Yes."

I glance down at her pregnant belly. "You're carrying Chance's child, aren't you?"

"That's none of your business."

"Why have you come, to flaunt yourself in my niece's face?"

"Because I loved Mr. Dells. He was kind to me like a father would be. I've come to pay my last respects. I have a right to do that. I have a right to that."

"You call this paying your last respects? I'm sure if Mr. Dells had known your situation, he would not have allowed you here." My tone is formal and as condescending as I can make it. The girl doesn't flinch.

"Mr. Dells knew because Chance told him," she says in a calm voice. "Dani is the only person who doesn't know. I think it's time she did."

"Don't call my niece by her name!" It's a silly thing to say considering the circumstances, but her familiarity is insulting.

"Don't tell me what to do." I am no threat, and she knows it. The real threat in our family is dead.

There is no sense in standing here. I step aside so she can pass, not sure what she will do or what else I can say. Whatever happens is out of my control. I notice that Dani and Chance are heading toward the office upstairs, and I am relieved by that. It is clear the woman wants some kind of confrontation, and Chance is determined she won't have it. She doesn't strike me as the kind of woman to keep things to herself, but why should she? If this is Chance's child, he is the one who has impregnated her; this child belongs to him as much as her. But how cruel of her to choose this day.

Jamison's hand is on my shoulder. "Lucille, we'd better start now," he says in the quiet, reassuring voice that has soothed our family through every sorrow we have had. What will he say about this, I wonder? "Chance told me not to wait for Dani. He said she is too upset. But Rose is here, and the boy. And you."

Rose has taken her seat in the front. She catches

my eye and nods toward the offices upstairs, where I know Chance has taken Dani. I glance back at Maria. Her eyes dart to her daughter but she can't let them settle.

"What will be, will be," I say quietly.

"I beg your pardon?" Jamison asks.

"Let's start now. Get this over with. Hilton said he wanted the memorial over quickly, so we should honor his wishes. This isn't so much for us as for the others who have come."

He leads me to the front row, stopping occasionally to allow those we pass to grab my hand and feel some connection with my brother. I am like some ancient queen walking through her kingdom.

"Such a good man."

"A credit to our community."

"A gift to the race!"

I nod to each, clasping hands as I move forward, barely hearing what they say.

When I get to my seat, I take Rose's hand in mine and she brings mine to her lips, rubbing it against her cheek like she used to do when she was younger. For some reason I think of Mel, and the pang of his loss even after all these years shoots through me.

"Where's Mommy?" Teddy's small voice brings me back to the present. "Why aren't they here?"

"They'll be here," I whisper to him, and then to Rose, "The bitch picked a helluva time to do this, didn't she?"

"You know, then?"

"I saw her outside."

"Pop planned to fire her next month. That was one of the last things he told me."

"Hilton knew about the pregnancy? Why the hell didn't somebody tell me?"

"Because you weren't involved, and you had enough on your mind with Pop's illness."

I shake my head half in disgust and half in sorrow. The act of a desperate woman, I think. As desperate as Maria Dells had once been.

"Where's Mommy?" Teddy asks again.

"She'll be here soon. Don't worry."

But Dani hasn't returned by the time the tributes begin or as Jamison praises his best and oldest friend, reciting yet again the stellar accomplishments of Hilton Dells and the company he founded, adding humorous anecdotes from their college days at Hampton. He calls for others to speak and so they do, from Isaac, the security guard, to Margaret Hanover, my brother's long-time secretary, with whom I'd always suspected he'd shared more than one lonely evening after his wife's departure.

It is easy to forget how important my brother

has been to so many people, as proud of him as if he'd been a member of their family. Some weep as they speak, bringing tears to my eyes.

When it is my turn to speak, Jamison helps me to the front of the room. I reach the podium, overwhelmed by the faces turned up in expectation. I take a breath and swallow deep, the way Hilton would tell me to do when I was a girl. I begin by telling what I know.

"I loved my brother dearly. He was the only parent I knew. He shaped me into becoming who I am," I say.

I recount our childhood, share my memories of the poverty we'd lived through and what it had taken for him to climb as far as he did. I speak from my heart, the honorable things that he did for me and for others that few people knew. I leave out the dishonorable things we never mention.

I end with the truth.

"My brother was a complicated man. He could be angry and bear grudges. He could be vindictive, but he could be loving, too. You had to know him well to understand how deep his feelings ran."

Dani comes out of the elevator and into the lobby as I finish. I assume she will join us, but suddenly she turns and runs out the door and from the building. Maria rises from her seat and follows her out.

I can't find my voice. I can't remember the words I planned to say. People shift uncomfortably. When words finally come, they aren't my own. Perhaps, they belong to Hilton, whispered when I need them. Or Annabel Dells.

"This is how it ends," I say. "There is no other way."

The room goes quiet.

"What did she say?" I hear someone in the front row whisper. "What did she mean by that?"

"Maybe that death gets us all sooner or later," someone answers in a low, amused voice. From somewhere, a youngster giggles.

Mercifully, Jamison quickly leads me to my seat. He takes things in hand then, thanking those who have come, ending the ceremony on a gracious note, and dispatching me, Rose, and Teddy into the waiting limousine that will carry us home for the repast.

Teddy is between us, his head in Rose's lap.

I look down to make sure he is asleep before I speak. "When did you find out?"

"Chance told me, then I talked it over with Pop before he died."

"Why didn't you tell Dani?"

"It wasn't my place to tell her." Her words are followed by a soft, sad smile. "Dani always seems to be the last person to know things. That's the advantage of being the baby of the family. Every-body looks out for you."

"What do you mean by that?"

Rose gazes out the window without answering, and I know from years of dealing with my brother's child that there is nothing more she will say. But she surprises me.

"I think I always knew that sooner or later, she would come back into our lives," she says.

"You saw Maria, then?"

"Who-calls-herself-Mariah?" she adds with a bitter chuckle. "When I first came in. She's changed so much. It hurt me to see how much she's changed."

"Did you speak to her?"

"No."

"Did you see her follow Dani out of the build-ing? What on earth can she possibly say to the child after all these years? Or to you?"

Rose gazes out the window in a strange, distant mood. I settle back into the soft comfort of the car, puzzled by her silence.

Dani

ten

*T*he hole is still there.
I thought it would close when she came back into
my life. I am surprised by how little I feel. For as
long as I can remember, I've fantasized about our
first meeting, the spontaneous embrace, the connection that I thought had been lost forever. I
would feel strong and whole because she had returned to me, I told myself.

But nothing within me has changed. I have a
vague curiosity about what she has done for all
those years and where she has been but that's all.
This middle-aged woman with her short, severe
haircut and dreary suit has no more connection to
me than someone I might glance at in the super-
market where she told me she worked. Rose's response to her when she saw her later that day was

quite different; her reaction was violent, and it stunned me.

When she said my name in the park, I knew I'd heard her voice before, I just wasn't sure where. My first response was irritation. I assumed she was some nosy busybody who had followed me over from the memorial, one of my father's employees who saw me bolt from the service in tears and, determined to honor his memory, taken it upon herself to comfort me. This woman's intrusion was unwanted.

"Dani," she said.

"Please go away. I'd like to be alone." I didn't bother to look at her. I didn't want a stranger to see me cry. Everything I felt—rage, humiliation, sorrow—was written on my face. It was not for the inspection of somebody who had no idea what had happened, what my husband had told me, what I had seen with my own eyes. I didn't want to be the subject of Monday morning gossip. I had seen Theresa's triumphant smile as I ran from the building. I had also seen the depth of my husband's shame.

"Coward," I could hear my dead father say as I ran away, his favorite word for someone who disappointed him.

"The hell with you, too!" I said to his memory.

"Dani."

"Go away!" I covered my face and I heard her step away. I wasn't sure where she had gone and didn't care. I assumed she had left the park, gone back to wherever the hell she'd come from. I had stopped crying by then and was on my cell phone with Ben. I needed to hear his voice, find the comfort I felt when I spoke to him.

"Ben, are you there? Where are you?"

He kept me waiting, dangling me, like he must have thought I had done to him. When he finally spoke he was distant and his voice was filled with tension. I had never heard him sound that way before.

"You told me Friday night it was over, Dani. Why are you doing this to me now?"

"Will you listen to what I have to say?" I spilled out what had happened with Chance, his betrayal, how I had run from the building. I'd made a mistake on Friday, I explained, my grief had clouded my thoughts and colored my words. He knew about grief, he said, there was nothing I could tell him about grief. I pleaded with him to see me again.

More moments of waiting. "I will always love you," he finally said. "Maybe in a year if you haven't worked things out with Chance we can see each other again, but I can't go through this thing again. You are no good for me, Dani. I told you that before. It's not any good. I have had too much pain in my life. I have to leave things behind that give me pain. I can't let you back in."

I was hurting so much, I wouldn't let myself hear what he had said. My first reaction was the anger of a spoiled rotten child, the one who makes an appearance when nothing else works, who won't go away no matter how old I get.

I told him to forget it, everything we had had was a lie anyway, and that he could go to hell along with everybody else because none of it was worth anything. I hung up the phone, sobbing like that angry child. Until she came again.

"Danielle," she said this time. No one had called me that since she left.

"Can I sit down?" I looked at her then, and my own face, thirty years older, stared back at me. "Yeah, it's me," she said with her crooked grin, then she took my hand and held it, gently like she used to, and she began to cry. I wasn't sure what to do, what reaction I should have. There were so many things I was feeling that I was numb. There was Chance. And Ben. My father's death. I didn't know her. There wasn't enough room for her. I simply let her hold my hand, let her cry, and said nothing.

"You remembered where we used to come," she said. "You remembered after all this time?" We were sitting on the same park bench we used to sit on when I was a child, I realized that when she said it. I always chose it. I had forgotten why.

"Yes," I said, but even as I said it, I knew the person who I used to come here with was gone forever. That had been somebody else, a woman who wore funny earrings, whose pretty hair I used to twirl around my fingers. I shifted away from her, leaving space between us.

"Why were you crying? Who made you cry?" she asked, using the same inflection she did when I was a child.

"Because of something that happened at my father's service." I was wary of her, unwilling to share an intimate part of myself. I couldn't bring myself to speak my father's name to her. She was a stranger. But at the same time there was a sense of familiarity. I felt strangely at ease with her, as if I was tied to her, and I could feel that string pulling somewhere inside my heart.

But I snatched my hand away anyway, the way I had from my father the day that he died when he had said her name. I thought of him then and something close to hate, a streak of it, went through me toward her.

"The little boy I saw you with. Was that your son, my grand—" She'd been on the verge of saying "grandson," then thought better of it. Aunt Lucille was Teddy's grandmother. She didn't have the right to claim him. I was glad she knew that.

"Yes. His name is Teddy."

"So you're married?"

"More or less," I said, which brought an unexpected smile, just a trace of the woman who used to be but then it disappeared.

"How old is he? Your son, I mean?"

"The same age I was when you left me," I said in a matter-of-fact way, and she flinched. I hadn't meant to hurt her; I didn't know her well enough for that. I was just stating the truth, like trees are green or rain is wet or sky is blue. The same age I was when you left me.

"I don't know what to say to you, Dani, after all this time, except that I have thought of you every day of my life. I dream about you at night. You and Rosie are the only reasons I am still alive. I'm not asking you to forgive me, but I needed to see you again. If this is the last time, then that is the way it will be. I know that you're safe, that you're happy and that is all I have ever hoped for."

They were pretty words, but it was as if a stranger had spoken them, read them from some script. I didn't let them enter my heart. They stayed outside. I wouldn't let them get inside. For her to come like she had, in the middle of what had happened, made no sense to me. I was going through it, but it felt unreal.

"What happened at Hilton's service to upset you so much?" she asked, and I stared at her, unsure of what to say.

"My husband betrayed me the way you betrayed my father."

The look that came into her eyes made me sorry I had said it like that, even though it was the truth. The way she dropped her head, closed her eyes as if my words had burned her. Suddenly I thought about my Aunt Lu, about what she says about grace and keeping it in one's life.

"But what is that?" I would ask her when I was a girl. "Something you do in church?"

"Grace is doing what is right and proper," she would tell me in her right and proper voice. "Softening yourself to someone's life. Acknowledging the spirit of another person, even if you're not sure they have one. That's as good a definition as any. It comes back at you, always."

And Aunt Lucille's idea of grace was what made me take hold of my mother's hand again. Hold it like she had held mine before, even though I didn't feel it, softening myself to her. Her eyes filled with so much gratitude even if I'd wanted to let her hand go, I couldn't. My aunt wouldn't let me.

"What was it like, where you were for all those years?" I asked. I could think of nothing else to say, and it seemed the logical next step in our conversation. What were your days like? How did you survive? How were you able to cope? They were the indifferent questions of a historian. My head always comes to my rescue when my heart is not sure where to go.

"In jail?" She was amused by my hesitancy to say the word, and again I caught a glimpse of the mother I remembered. Just a bit, in the twinkle of her eye. But then her shoulders dropped as if some weight had fallen upon them.

"I'll tell you what made it tolerable. My memories of you and Rose. A good book in the library whose pages have not been torn or soiled. Shielding some young girl from evilness—and there was evil in that place, but more good than you could imagine.

"You block things out there. The days are indistinguishable—you hardly notice them passing except for their dullness. Boredom is what you fight. Constant, ever-present boredom. So you learn to look forward to small things. Sunlight glimpsed through a cloud, an extra piece of pie or candy, good thread to sew your blouse, a ribbon to wear in your hair." She laughed; it was a light, lovely sound that jarred my memory.

"The best thing about prison is that you get out. I did my time. I have my freedom. I deserve to live now. I try to think about it as little as possible. You're the first person I've even talked to about it. The very first."

"You don't have any friends?"

She shifted uncomfortably. "Trish is dead. Do you remember Trish?" I shook my head and she sighed. That sigh told me more than I wanted to know. There were years of anguish in that breath, years of sorrow that I didn't want to feel.

"I keep to myself," she said, then changed the subject. "Did you get my letters? I wrote you every day. Not a holiday, birthday, weekend went by that I didn't write you and Rose, every day all the time I was there. I wrote, even when I was getting out. You never got them, did you?"

"No," I said.

She drew in breath, then let it go, and I thought about what Ben told me once about the day his family had been killed. All he could do was breathe, he said. Take in one breath at a time. Let it go. Wait for the next, then the next, until the day was done and he could take the pills that would let him sleep a deep, dreamless sleep until the next morning. He had wanted to die, and he nearly did, but his mother and sister kept him live. Caring for him, cooking for him, making sure he lived until the next day. So many times, he thought of killing himself, he said, but to die would give death a victory, and he wasn't yet ready to bestow that reward. He had to live *because* they had died. So he took in a breath, one more, drawn in slowly, then released, and he lived.

I wondered if my mother had done that, all those days one breath at a time, keeping alive for Rose and me.

"I wrote you," I said. When I said it, I recalled those carefully worded letters as if I'd written them yesterday.

"I got them. Every single one. The guards would bring them to me, the only thing I lived for were your letters. I kept them all. I'll show them to you someday. If you want to see them. Every single one. But then they stopped coming."

"I'm sorry."

"No," she said. "I knew that you were grown by then."

"Yes, I was."

So we sat there, the two of us, in the park where we used to go, and when it started to rain, she asked me if I was ready to leave, and I told her I didn't want to go home. She asked me if I wanted to come to her place, apologizing for it before we got there. I said I didn't have my car, and she said we could take a bus. That was how she had come. It would take awhile, but maybe it would give us a chance to talk.

But we don't talk on the bus to her home. I stare out the window, uncomfortably aware of this woman who sits so close to me, of the way her hip feels next to mine as the bus lurches at each stop. I try to find her in my memory, place her now as she was then, but she isn't to be found. The new one is here, and I realize that the old one is gone forever, except in my dreams.

I think of other things, Teddy and the way Chance had wept when we made love the night before, about Ben and what he said about his pain. Sometimes there is too much pain to bear and you simply have to let it go. He had let me go. If I got to know her better, would I end up doing the same with her, my mother?

"Are you hungry, Dani? We can pick up something on the way home. I don't think I have anything in the house," she says as we get off the bus. So we stop in a store and she buys the makings for spaghetti. I offer to pay but she won't let me.

Her apartment building is shabby. I try not to notice the holes in the wall as we walk upstairs, how cramped and dark the apartment is that she leads me into. The furnishings are old, secondhand, and the place has a bad smell to it. She opens the window to let in some air. A drunken brawl plays out in the apartment next door, kids scream loudly on the sidewalk outside.

"How long have you lived here?" I make my voice neutral.

"About a year, I was in a halfway house for a while, and then they helped me find this place. It's not much, is it?" She smiles when she says it, letting me know that it is all right to feel the way I do. I wonder if she can tell what I am thinking. I'd always assumed that when I was a little girl. "I wish I had a better place to bring you, after all these years." She turns away, ashamed. "I still remember your father's house. Is it still as grand as it used to be?"

"Yes. My Aunt Lucille lived with us and took care of it after—" She doesn't give me a chance to finish the sentence.

"Lucille brought you and Rosie up, then?"

"Yes." My tone is short. I am unwilling to discuss my aunt with her.

"She never liked me much, your aunt."

"She had good reason not to."

"I wish—" She stops, turning away.

The silence is awkward. She is as uncomfortable as I am.

"I'm happy to be here," I say because I know she needs to hear it. *Grace.* I can hear my aunt whispering the word in my ear. Be generous, Dani. Be gracious. If I taught you anything, I taught you that!

"Thank you," she says. "I'd better put on dinner." She escapes into the kitchen to start the meal.

"Can I help you do something?" I call out. It sounds fake, like something on TV. But that is all you have sometimes, clichés and bullshit.

"Just sit here with me. Just stay."

I sit down on one of the wobbly chairs in the small kitchen and watch her cook like I must have done when I was a kid. When she is finished, we sit at the small table and eat in silence. After she washes the dishes, she brings out the letters she has saved. There are more than I remembered, all written in childish script with the colored pencils I'd borrowed from Rose. They're as fragile as ancient documents, faded around the edges, folded countless times. Their value to her is clear. I handle them carefully, touched that she's kept them, then watch her wrap them in the toilet paper that she'd saved them in and put them away.

"Will Rose come if you ask her?" I can see the longing in her eyes.

"I'm sure she will," I say. Rose is far more generous with time and people than me. There would be no reason why she wouldn't. I wonder if my sister's connection to her will be stronger than mine. Rose is older, after all. She'd had more time to know her. But we have rarely talked about her as adults. I had spoken about my mother to God in my prayers. I don't know if Rose had.

"Did Rose ever write you?"

"No."

There is tension between us now. I wonder why it has come so suddenly.

"Can I make a few calls?" She nods toward the bedroom where I can have some privacy. "I want to let my aunt know where I am. I'll call Rose, too."

I go into her bedroom and close the door, happy to get away. Settling down on her bed, I call my aunt.

"Dani? Where are you? Are you all right? Where have you been? What's going on with Chance?" The questions tumble out of her mouth in one breath. I can almost see her thin frame trembling, her left hand propped on her hip, her right hand jabbing the air with a cigarette. The image makes me laugh.

"What in the world are you laughing about?"

"Because I love you so much!" I'd heard that voice so many times when I'd been a teenager, coming back drunk from hanging out with Cassie, high as shit, knowing Aunt Lu could smell wine and weed on my breath. My eyes always giving me away, me not giving a damn.

"Where the heck are you?"

"I'm fine, Aunt Lu."

"I asked where you are."

"I'm with my—Maria." *Maria who calls herself Mariah.* I couldn't get the word out, couldn't call her "mother" to my aunt, who had earned that title.

She pauses. "I saw her leave with you. What happened?"

"I'll tell you later."

"Later? I want to know now!"

"Why are you so impatient, Aunt Lu!"

"*Where* are you? I know you're with her, but *where* are you?"

"Winston Street."

"Winston Street?"

"In an apartment on the fourth floor. Four hundred and twenty-five Winston. Down past the old mill."

"That's the worst neighborhood in the whole damn city! I'm coming to get you."

That's my aunt, as frail as she is, still my protector and willing with a moment's notice to brave the wilds of Winston Street. The thought of her, arms flailing, pressed hair flying, brings tears to my eyes.

"No, you're not. I'm fine. I'll be home later."

"Rose and I were worried half to death about you!"

"I'm sorry. I didn't mean to worry you."

"The hell you didn't." I hear the lighter click as she lights the next one. "At least you're okay."

Another phrase from my teenage years. At least. At least you're not dead, maimed, arrested.

"How did things go?" I ask about the memorial. I'd almost forgotten about it. It didn't seem as if it had been the same day.

"Fine. We missed you, though. I was so worried about you!"

"I love you, Aunt Lu. I love you so much."

She's not as tough as you think, Rose had told me

the day my father died, and she was right. My aunt was never as tough as I thought she was.

"I love you, too. You're okay, now," she says like she has for as long as I can remember. Just hearing her say it like she did told me that I was. "But it's time for you to come home."

"Where is Teddy?"

"Chance took Teddy home. I told Teddy that you were upset about Hilton's death and you needed time alone. He nodded his head like an old man, like he understands everything in the world, and said he hoped you were okay. You've raised a sweet child, Dani. You and Chance."

She added Chance because I hadn't mentioned him, and she wanted to get a read on how I was feeling. I wasn't sure myself.

"Randa made dinner for both of them, and she and her husband, Brent, I think that's his name, stayed with the two of them until Chance put the boy to bed. He didn't say what he told your neighbors. Probably the same thing I told Teddy.

"But you've got to come home, Dani. You know that, don't you? You can wait before you make a final decision, but you have to come home because your son needs you."

I'd figured out that much. I knew now what had happened between Chance and Theresa, but I didn't know if I had it in me to forgive him. I'm not sure about anything anymore.

"Do you want to bring Teddy back here, to the house, and stay with me while you figure things out?"

"That might be a good idea."

"I can call Chance and have him bring the boy home for a few days. He loves coming here, and we can pretend it's like a vacation."

"No, Aunt Lu. I'll tell him the truth."

It strikes me again how quickly things you took for granted ten minutes before can change forever. I had been so sure of everything on Friday night. So secure in my life when I put Teddy to bed, made love to Chance, said good-bye to Ben. Words are easy to say. It's what comes after them that's tough.

"Is Rose still there, let me talk to her." My aunt puts down the phone and calls Rose. The two of them talk a moment before Rose's voice comes on the line.

"Dani, so you're with her now? What are you doing there?" Rose's voice is strained and tense.

"She wants to know if you will come. She wants to see you." I can't say "our mother." "She" will do for now.

I give her the address, and she says she will be over as soon as she can.

Maria is sitting on the couch, gazing out the window when I return to the living room. I tell her that Rose is coming, and she nods.

"Thank you, Dani," she says.

She asks if I'd like some coffee and puts on water. I hear her bang the top of the jar of instant coffee on the table so she can screw it off. When I was a child, she hated instant coffee.

She brings in two mugs, and we sit on the couch waiting for Rose to come. Her eyes fasten on the door. We wait for an hour.

"Rosie!" she calls out when the bell finally rings, and she jumps up to open it. Rose looks as if she doesn't recognize her, then she slaps her hard across the face.

When my mother left, she took different things from each of us. I understood only what she ripped from me, and what my Aunt Lucille, in her own peculiar way, had managed to put back. I didn't understand yet what Rose had lost, what she gave and what she was given. I just knew at that moment that there was unfinished business between them.

Rose

eleven

ose! What is wrong with you? Why did you slap her like that?" Dani screams, stepping in front of Maria to protect her.

I knew why I'd done it: for not loving us enough and leaving us as she had. For bringing *him* into our lives. For the overwhelming guilt of a seventeen-year-old that had wormed itself inside me. I felt nothing but relief when I hit her. A chapter ended. A debt repaid. I couldn't hear my sister's voice any better than I'd heard hers on the day that it happened.

She stands there as if she deserves it, taking it the way she did his blows that afternoon. Her terrified eyes stare back at me. I drop my hand, ashamed that I've brought that look into her eyes again, brought that day back.

"Rosie!" She places her hand on her face, then

moves toward me, tries to take me in her arms. I allow her to embrace me, breast to breast, as I had the last time I saw her. I let her hold me for a moment, then pull away. I can't find it in me to call her "Mother."

I remember what Marshall said earlier, that seeing her again was inevitable, that coming to terms with, then accepting and forgiving your parents for who they are and what they'd done was essential to becoming an adult. Up until this point, I'd thought I'd passed that threshold. But I've paid a price for my secrets.

I try to think of something wise and comforting to say to Dani. My first impulse is always that of caretaker, to offer comfort and kindness as I do to my students. But there is nothing to say; my actions speak louder than any words. Rationally, I know Maria isn't to blame. She made the only decision she thought she could make that day. But knowing and feeling what is right are quite different things, and no matter what I know, I can't let my feelings go.

"Come here, Rosie. Come here to me." Her voice is small and fearful and makes me sigh with sadness. I step inside her apartment. It is a dismal little place, which makes me feel sorry for her and that my reaction had been what it was. I can smell spaghetti, which she must have cooked for Dani. Two blue coffee mugs are on the wooden chest that serves as a coffee table. Outside the open window, I hear the voices of kids, still playing in the street even though it's after nine. I'd seen them when I came into the building. One of them, a little girl with cornrowed hair, whom I recognized as one of my third-graders, had run to greet me.

"You here to see my mama, Dr. Dells?" She'd grabbed my hand, and we walked toward the building together.

"No, baby, not tonight," I said. *I'm here to see my own*, I'd thought. "What are you doing out here at this time of night?" I put on the halfhearted scowl I pull out for my students.

"Playing, Dr. Dells. Nighttime is the right time!" she said with a naughty little giggle, then ran into the building before I could catch her, which made me chuckle. This is a neighborhood touched by hardscrabble lives and backbreaking poverty, the kind my father had known as a child. I saw the life my father had lived when I visited the homes of my kids. I know the desperation they face by sight, sound, and smell.

So this is where Maria has ended up.

She reaches for me again, trying to embrace me, and I step back into the hall, like some scared kid; one hug is enough. Dani grabs my arm and gently pulls me into the room. She is puzzled and alarmed by the way I'm acting. Her eyes search mine for an answer. I have none to give.

Perhaps I should explain what I am feeling, how in an instant the sight of this woman has thrown me back nearly twenty-five years into the worst night of my life, and that I'm surprised how fresh my anger still is.

I consider apologizing for my behavior. You just don't walk into someone's house and slap her in the face. The woman is more than twenty years older than me. The same age as my aunt. That alone should have restrained me. Yet it didn't.

She offers me dinner. I politely refuse. She is trying to please me. I don't want to be won over.

"Will you have something to drink, Rosie? Some coffee. I have some gin. Maybe a drink—"

"Water is fine," I say, still wary.

I sit down next to Dani on the couch. When she brings in the water, I notice she's put a lemon slice in the glass, which is the way I used to like it when I was a little girl.

"No lemon," I say and take it out.

"I'm sorry." Her face is still red from my slap. "Do you want me to bring you some more?"

"No. I'm not that thirsty." I take a few swallows and hand it back to her.

"Are you sure?"

"Yes, I'm fine."

She takes the glass back into the kitchen, and I hear her emptying the water into the sink. She begins to take the dishes off the drying rack, and I hear her opening and closing cabinets, putting things from dinner back into the refrigerator.

"That was a terrible thing to do, slapping her like that," Dani scolds me again in a whisper. "She doesn't mean us any harm. She showed me all the letters I'd written her when she was in prison. She kept every single one, wrapped in toilet paper. Can you imagine that? It made me so sad! Can you just be nice to her for a little while, and then we can leave."

"Okay," I say.

"I'm going to come and help you," Dani calls out to her, and goes into the kitchen to help her put the dishes away. I sit for a moment or two and then wander into her small bedroom. It is dark outside, but the bedroom shades are still up. I consider pulling them down, but change my mind; they aren't my responsibility. For all I know, she may prefer them up. A Bible lies on a table near the bed, and I open it. It belonged to her mother, Mai, whose name is written with an ornate flourish. I sit down on her bed, suddenly very tired. The mattress is cheap, as cheap as the one we both knew so well.

* * *

When I saw her at my father's memorial my heart beat so fast, it frightened me. The last thing any of us needed was for me to drop dead of a heart attack on the day we put him away. Too many things were happening at once. I couldn't take it all in. Dani's crisis with Chance. Teddy's feelings to soothe. My aunt to reassure. So I'd pulled out my gracious public persona and gone through the motions.

I wondered what my reaction would be if I had to actually confront her. I assumed it would be indifference. A cool detachment. I understand the workings of the mind well enough to know I should have been prepared for anger, even though I've always been good at concealing it.

I didn't intend to confront her.

So I rode home from the memorial service with my aunt and when we got home, attended to our social obligations: making sure the food was properly served, advising the bartender to be restrained in his pouring, graciously greeting our guests and thanking them for coming. Friends whom I hadn't seen for years stopped by, as well as politicians and employees whom I barely knew. Word had spread that my father had left his business to his daughters, and everybody wanted to know what we were going to do. Marshall came in with a contingent of teachers and principals from our district. I was happy to see him and relieved that he didn't bring his wife.

"Are you okay?" he whispered as soon as he could get me alone. I nodded toward my father's study, and he followed me in as soon as he could make a graceful getaway. When he was inside, I closed the door and we embraced, holding each other tightly, which in itself was exciting because it was the first time we'd touched intimately outside of our room. He kissed the tip of my nose, which he loves to do, and then my lips, gently parting them with his tongue.

"Thank you for coming," I said.

"You didn't answer me. How are you doing?"

"Okay, more or less."

"Mostly more or mostly less?"

"Less. It's been awful. Dani's disappeared. I have no idea where she is, and then of all the damned things to happen, my mother showed up. She was sitting in the back of the building. I saw her when I came in."

He took me in his arms again. "Did anyone else see her?"

"My aunt. She's changed so much I don't think anybody else would have recognized her. Except Dani, maybe."

"It was inevitable. You know that, don't you?"

I nodded that I did.

"What did she say?"

"I didn't speak to her."

He gave me a slight, ironic smile. "You'll have to talk to her sooner or later. Do you know how to find her?"

"Dani is probably with her now. She was upset and ran out of the service. My mother followed her. Sooner or later, Dani will get in touch with me, I'm sure of that, and I'll take it from there. So today, of all days, my past finally catches up with me."

"The past has a way of doing that."

We held each other awhile longer, and then he let me go. It made me feel strong to be with him. I hadn't realized how much I needed that strength.

"Do you know what else is inevitable?" he said after a moment. "Our relationship. We have to come to terms with that, Rose. You mean too much to me to keep hiding it."

"I know," I said, the first time I admitted it to myself.

"I want you to call me if you see her. I don't want us to wait until next Friday. I need to know what happens."

I was frightened for a moment. I was losing control, but there was no control anymore anyway. I had to trust that things would take their own course, whatever that would be.

There was a hurried knock on the door. We stepped further apart as Aunt Lucille rushed into the study. Marshall, now the respectable principal, introduced himself and shook my aunt's hand. I noticed a bit of lipstick on his upper lip and the top of his shirt. I was sure my sharp-eyed aunt had spotted it, but knew she had the good sense not to say anything, at least in front of him. Aunt Lu glanced at me with a trace of a smile, then grew serious.

"You'll have to excuse us, Mr. Webster. I have to talk with my niece."

Marshall gave me a polite nod and left. I faced Aunt Lu, preparing myself to face her suspicions, but that was the last thing on her mind.

"Have you heard from Dani?"

"No. I've called her twice, but she didn't answer her cell."

"What should we do, Rose? I don't know what to do!" She dropped onto the couch, shaking her head in distress. I remembered suddenly the last time I'd been in this study. It had been with my father, the day before his stroke. I remembered his anger at Chance, softened only by his concern for Dani. The sharpness of his image brought tears to my eyes. I turned away so my aunt couldn't see what was in them.

"Call her again, now!" Aunt Lu ordered and I did for her benefit, but it was to no avail.

"She'll call me when she's ready," I said, my thoughts on my father again, the grief I'd managed not to feel suddenly coming over me.

"I don't trust Maria Dells," my aunt said.

"She's not to be trusted," I said, realizing as I said them that they were my father's words, not mine. I still carried his anger inside me. "We're grown women now, Aunt Lu. There's nothing she could do to hurt either one of us," I added.

Aunt Lucille nodded that she understood.

"What a terrible day this has been," she said, and I agreed with her.

We returned to talk to our guests, concealing our worry as best we could. Chance and Teddy were there by then. I hugged Teddy and ignored Chance, thinking even as I did that I'd never seen a man look so forlorn.

Three hours later, Dani did call, and I'd driven to the address that she gave me, parked the car, fastened the Club to my steering wheel, and walked toward the building, not sure what I would do when I saw her. I'd greeted my little student, trudged up the stairs, then slapped the mother I hadn't seen in over twenty years square in the face.

She comes in now, and sits down beside me on the bed.

"The last time I saw you, it was in a bedroom like this," I say, looking her in the eye, the first time I'd done it since I'd been there. She doesn't say anything to that, just gazes down at the faded yellow bedspread and the braided rug on the floor.

"How do you keep anger burning so long, Rose?"

"I didn't realize it was still in me until I saw you."

"It's your father's anger, too?"

"Some of it," I say, and she nods that she understands. "Why did you make me promise to lie that night? Did you have any idea how much that lie would cost me?"

"You didn't lie."

"Of course I did!" I stare at her in disbelief, amazed that she couldn't see it the way it had been. "I lied by omission, by not telling the whole truth."

"I didn't have a choice."

"If I'd stayed with you, told them what had happened that day, they would have understood, they would have been more lenient with you."

Her response comes slowly, thoughtfully, as if she had considered it for a long time, and knew exactly what she was going to say. "If it had come out that you were there, a seventeen-year-old girl, that you were even indirectly involved, it would have been worse for all of us. *You* would have been the one in those newspaper stories and on TV. You would never have lived it down. Your life could never have been normal again, and it would have made us both into freaks.

"I killed Durrell. I got what I deserved. Please tell me that you understand that now. Please say that to me now."

I turn away, not sure what to feel or believe. I don't want to hear her beg me. "I ended up feeling responsible for what happened to you and for his death."

"How could you feel responsible for his death?" She touches my cheek like she used to do when I was a little girl. I pull away.

"You killed him because of me, and I had to keep that inside me. My holding back the truth, my part in the whole thing sent you to jail." My voice is trembling. I don't want to cry. I swore to myself I wouldn't.

"I brought him into our lives. He raped you. He deserved to die."

I am surprised by the hardness that comes over her—the conviction in her eyes, the firm resolution of her voice. How could she have gone all these years and not known the truth?

"You thought he raped me? He didn't rape me. It didn't mean anything to me one way or the other. You gave it meaning, not me."

"You were seventeen."

"I knew what I was doing."

She doesn't say anything for a long time, just sits there, staring at the bedspread, then closes her eyes.

"Are you sure it wasn't jealousy that made you pull that trigger?" It is the question that I never admitted I had until I say it.

"I don't know anymore," she says.

She weeps, and I put my arm around her, amazed how fragile and weak she is. Dani comes into the room then. I'd almost forgotten she was there.

"What happened that day? When Durrell Alexander was killed?" Dani asks.

"It's over and done with," I say.

"Tell me! I have a right to know."

She sits down on the bed then, edging between us like she used to do when she was a little girl, and together we tell her everything we remember.

twelve

You're that girl I saw on the street, aren't you?" Durrell Alexander asked me that first day.

I didn't expect him to open the door. I'd finally gotten the nerve to confront you, and I'd assumed you'd be there when I rang the bell. I'd walked past the apartment building a dozen times and even stood in the lobby once, but had never gone up the six flights of stairs to the apartment. I was out of breath by the time I reached the door.

He must have seen a hundred girls on the street on any number of days, but he remembered me, and that made me happy.

"I don't know what you're talking about," I said.

His smile told me I knew *exactly* what he was talking about. It was an easygoing, charming smile that you had to return because it looked so harmless. His question knocked me off balance; the smile knocked me back on. That "day" was now our connection, and I was flattered the way any seventeen-year-old girl probably would be who has been noticed and remembered by an older man.

"I came to see my mother."

"Your mother's not here."

"Where is she?"

"I don't know."

"When is she coming back?"

"Don't know that either." He looked me over for a minute, then said, "You look like you're about to pass out, kid. You want to come in and get something to drink, some water, a Coke?" He stepped out of the way so that I could come in.

I hesitated before I went in.

I've often wondered how different all our lives would have turned out if I'd turned down his invitation.

"No, thank you," I could have said, because I was always a polite girl. "Just tell my mother I came to see her, that I miss her, that I want her to come back to us," I could have said, and that would have been that. You would have come back in a couple of months. He would have gone on to make his films. Nobody would have been the wiser.

Or I could have said nothing at all, hightailed it

out while I still had the chance. Why did I step into an apartment with a man I didn't know for a drink I didn't even want?

What was going through my head?

It was that same sense of mischief that made me swipe lace panties from Bloomingdale's. The adventurous spirit that urged me to take one more chance. The good little girl gone naughty, turning cartwheels on the wrong side of the road.

I was curious about him, this man that you had run off with. What did he have that was so irresistible, that had made you leave us, whom I knew you loved, without looking back? What was his magic?

It was a hot Saturday, thick with humidity, the second week in August. Pop was away on a business trip; Dani and Aunt Lu had left early for the Jersey Shore. I told them I was going to spend the day with a friend, and I'd intended to do it, but then started thinking about you, boarded the bus to the city, and taken the subway uptown.

He left it up to me. There was no coercion, just a simple question requiring a simple answer. Yet I hesitated.

"Well—" he said. He shrugged, preparing to close the door, and I stepped in.

It was a narrow hall, and I followed him into the living room. I sat down on the couch. He brought me water that he took from a bottle in the refrigerator. I heard him unscrewing the top. Neither of us spoke. He was typing something on a noisy old typewriter, and he went back to it. I sipped my water and watched him as he worked. I thought he had forgotten I was there.

"Why don't you get a computer?" I asked. Pop had brought one from his office, and I was learning how to use it. I was toying with the idea of majoring in computer science in college.

"I can't afford one." He glanced up, slightly annoyed.

"Do you know when she'll be back?"

"Who?"

"Who do you think? The person I came here to see."

He shrugged his shoulders. "Your guess is as good as mine." He was intent upon concentrating on whatever he was doing.

"Did she know you were coming over here?" he asked while he worked.

"No."

He glanced up then. "Did you know that she came to see you and your sister?"

"When?" I didn't try to hide my excitement about that.

"Couple of months ago."

My heart jumped.

"I think your old man had the locks changed, that's what she said, anyway."

"Well, thanks for that useful bit of information," I snapped.

He looked up then. "Sorry. I thought you knew."

"How would I know if nobody told me!"

We sat there for a while, me drinking the water and watching him in silence.

"You finish that water yet?" he asked.

I gulped it down. "What are you doing?"

"Writing."

"What are you writing?"

He looked up then. "Your mother never told you what I do for a living?"

I shook my head. I was curious. I'd had no idea why Durrell Alexander existed except to steal you, and for the first time since he'd glanced at me on the street that day, his gaze lingering on my body and in my mind longer than it should have, Durrell became a real person for me.

"I make movies. I'm a filmmaker. I'm working out the treatment for an idea I have."

"You mean like *Shaft* or something?" Those were the years of black action movies, and that was the first one that came to mind.

"No," he said, shaking his head with a slight smile. "Not like *Shaft* or something."

"What, then?"

"I'll let you know when I'm finished."

I took the glass, rinsed it out in the sink in the

kitchen, and put it on the dish rack. He leaned back in his chair and watched me walk across the room.

"You ever been a dancer?"

"No."

"You move like one, did you know that, all smooth and graceful."

"I took ballet when I was a kid. So do you."

"So do I, what?"

"Move like a dancer." That startled him, and he stopped short, giving me a look that I wasn't sure how to interpret, followed with a burst of laughter.

"So when have you ever seen me move?"

"A couple of times," I said, going back to the couch, sitting down.

The sun was shining brightly through the open window, throwing afternoon light on the room. I got up and walked around, picking up items at random and putting them down again like a child in a store, picking up things like I used to do before I would steal them.

I saw one of your copper earrings, picked it up, held it for a moment, then slipped it into my pocket. I opened a newspaper, read a few pages, put it down where I'd gotten it, then went through the paperbacks jammed on one of the wobbly bookshelves. A dog-eared copy of *Native Son* caught my eye. "We had this in lit class," I said.

"You must have gone to a good school," he said.

There was a huge bureau that looked like it belonged in a bedroom. The handles on the drawers were shaped like lions, jaws opened, looking like they might bite. They gave me the creeps. A gun lay on top of the bureau. I assumed it was a toy. I'd never seen a real gun before, and couldn't imagine somebody leaving a real one lying around like that. I picked it up and held it for a moment; the urge was irresistible.

"Hey, put that down!" He stood up, yelling like a parent as he came over to where I was standing.

"Is it loaded?"

"Of course it's loaded! Never play with guns, didn't your daddy teach you that?" he said as he carefully took it out of my hands.

"Why do you keep a gun around anyway?'

"It's an heirloom. It belonged to my father."

"Your father?" It hadn't occurred to me that this stealer of mothers could actually come from somewhere. He must have read my face; my expression made him chuckle.

"Yeah, I've got one, too. Would you believe that?"

"How come it's loaded?"

"There's been a couple of break-ins in the building. I cleaned it last night and loaded it in case I ever need to use it," he added. "I usually don't keep it out." He put it in the top drawer of the bureau and slammed it shut.

"What's your name, anyway?"

"She never told you?"

"No, you tell me." His voice had a teasing edge to it. Maybe that was just for me, or maybe that was just the way he talked to women. I wasn't sure then, and I'm not sure now.

"Rose."

"Rose. I remember now. The oldest."

"What did she tell you about me?"

"Not much," he said, lighting a cigarette, then offering the pack to me. I took one, and he lit it for me.

I was used to smoking with friends, stale Salems secretly inhaled in the cool of somebody's back bedroom. I didn't do it regularly enough to be hooked, and nicotine still had an effect on me. I felt light-headed, dizzy, so I sat back down on the couch. Durrell went back to his desk, worked awhile longer, than glanced up as if just remembering I was there again.

"Time to go home, kid," he said.

"I told you I'm waiting for my mother."

He pulled back from the typewriter. "Your mother's not coming back. I don't think she lives here anymore."

"What do you mean, you don't think she lives here anymore?"

"Just what I said."

"Where does she live, then?'

"Hell if I know. You don't believe me? Go look

in the bedroom. I put the rest of her clothes in that black plastic bag on the floor. Whenever the hell she comes back she can get them. You want to take it with you?"

I glanced toward the bedroom but didn't go in. "How come you didn't tell me that in the first place?"

He looked up. "Maybe I'm enjoying your company."

"Right," I said.

"Don't sell yourself short. You're smart, you're cute . . . but it's time to go home, baby doll. I got work to do." He turned back to his desk, started to type again.

"When I see her, I'll tell her you came by. She took most of her stuff when she left, but sooner or later she's going to come back for the rest," he said as if he were talking to himself.

"How come you're so sure?"

"I just am."

"Do you want her to come back?"

He glanced up at me. "You remind me of me when I was a kid, you know that? Questions. Questions. Questions. Always questions about shit that is none of your business. Go!" He pointed toward the door.

"Okay, already," I said. I slammed the door hard when I left.

But I knew I would be back. It was that last quick glance before I closed the door on him, sitting behind his desk, pounding away so purposefully on that broken-down old typewriter, oblivious to everything but his work.

If things hadn't turned out as they did, Durrell Alexander would have been just one more exciting teenage adventure for me, somewhere between stealing underwear and making love to my best friend's cousin from Morehouse in the back seat of his daddy's Jag.

But I was curious as always, so the next week around the same time, I rang his doorbell again.

I understand now what I was up to. I see it in the kids in my school. Girls grow up much faster now than they did twenty years ago. Sexual experimentation and promiscuity start much younger, thirteen, twelve, eleven with some kids. I had a case three weeks ago where we caught a nine-year-old giving head to a ten-year-old boy in the janitor's closet. Twelve is the new seventeen, and this new sexual derring-do is the bane of every teacher in my school.

I've done a lot of reading, talked to experts, and even given seminars on the subject of teenage sexuality. I'm considered almost an expert on it now. I can tell at a glance what some sexually mature twelve-year-old is up to. I can spot the game of seduction that young girls like to play, turning on a man, preferably someone older, for the pure and simple joy of doing it. Puppies tearing up somebody's shoe to feel the strength of those sharp new teeth.

He was surprised to see me. "You're back?"

"Yeah." I jutted my chin out defiantly.

"She's still not here."

"Maybe I enjoyed your company."

He gave a half-smile because most women did.

"How old are you anyway?"

"Eighteen." I *would* be eighteen soon. I *felt* eighteen, and that was what was important. It was *almost* the truth, and what was my small lie compared to the ones *you* had told?

"You sure about that?" Something in my tone made him suspect a lie. He knew enough about women to know when they were lying and why.

"I swear on my grandmother's grave," I said. Grandmother Mai meant nothing to me.

"That sounds pretty serious," he said.

"It is. I adored my grandmother."

He believed me, and I believe if I'd told the truth, he would have slammed the door in my face. But maybe not. After all these years, I'm still not sure what kind of a man Durrell really was.

I came in, sat down on the couch, watched him study me.

"So why are you *really* here?"

"I wanted to find out something."

"Find out what?"

"What my mother sees in you."

"Saw in me." He emphasized the past tense. "Our thing is over. She'll be back with the three of you before the year is out." He shrugged his shoulders, shaking things off, as if he didn't give a damn. "So what do you think she saw in me?" That teasing edge was in his voice, which made me smile.

Little girl trying to be big. Flirting with her mama's boyfriend. Wandering into the forbidden land.

I'm not sure who seduced whom. I just know that there was nothing innocent about it on my part. I was angry, I know that, at you, at him, and a bit at myself for being there. It was my way of getting back at you, getting even. And maybe he was right, that you might be back with us soon, and if you found out this, I could be sure you would.

Besides, you'd left him anyway. Or so he said.

The idea of it was actually more thrilling than the act itself. I'd slept with enough boys my own age to know what to expect. I viewed having sex with Durrell as experimental, performed with a certain objectivity. Like in biology class when you cut open a calf's lung, you almost don't think of it as a calf.

I wondered what kind of lover he would be. And now I was going to find out.

"So let me get this straight. You came all the way over here again, braved the wilds of the Number Two train, all the way up those stairs, to find out what your mother sees in me?"

"Yeah." I jutted out my chin a little further, tough little girl playing sexy. It was a game, and he was playing, too.

"So do you want me to show you?" He smiled slightly, but there was something in his eyes. Not amusement, I'm sure of that. Maybe a bit of sorrow. I still don't know what to make of it.

"Yeah."

From the moment I heard his voice on the phone, there had been that sexual tension. I let myself enjoy it.

I undressed in the living room, dropping my clothes into a pile on the floor. He watched me without speaking, his eyes following each piece of clothing as it hit the floor. I felt like a striptease artist, and I was thrilled by the way his eyes followed my movements—like a scene out of *Modern Romance* or one of my romances.

We went into his dark, hot room. He opened a window, lit some incense. Jasmine, I still remember the too-sweet, flowery smell. I became an interested, aroused observer.

Dreamlike. That was what it was. I was used to the passion of boys my own age, their fast, awkward strokes and diffident touch, but he was sure of himself, a man who knew women's bodies well, and with his fingers, palms, tongue he quickly learned mine.

"Do you want to go on?" He touched the inside of my ear with his tongue when he whispered.

"Yeah." Same word. Same tone. Same attitude. Even as I said it, I wondered what I was trying to prove.

I reached an orgasm quickly; I always did. I got out of bed. He reached for a cigarette.

"So, Rose." When he said my name, his voice was gentle and as curious as I had been. I was surprised by how tender he sounded. "Did you find out what you wanted to know?"

That made me laugh, the way he said it. "Yeah, I guess you could say that." Then we both laughed, a joke between us, at the expense of you because your presence had been there from the first. He got out of bed and walked toward me, kissed me lightly on my lips and forehead. I was dressed by then, and there was an ease between us.

"You're not a virgin, are you?"

"Or course not. You think I'd want you to be my first?"

"Good. I wouldn't want to be your first! Nor your last either, for that matter. But it was good."

"Yeah, and don't worry, you won't be my last."

He chuckled. "That's good," he said. "You don't want to shower or anything, you can—"

"I'll take one when I get home." Oddly enough, showering in his presence seemed a more intimate act than having sex.

"Do you mind if I do?"

I shrugged my shoulders. "No, go ahead."

I went back into the living room and waited for him to finish. He came out dressed.

"How old are you ?" I asked him.

"Older than you."

"You're younger than my mother, aren't you."

"Yeah. Five or six years. But let's not talk about your mother." He lit another cigarette. "So where are you off to now, Miss Rose?"

"Home."

"Let me walk you to the train."

"I can walk myself."

"Come on. Don't be like that," he said, and we headed out the door. We didn't talk much as we walked to the subway. There wasn't any tension or anger between us, there was nothing. I'm not sure what either of us felt, and at that moment I felt older than he did. I felt sorry for him. I felt sorry for you both.

"So what happened between you and my mother?" I asked as the train came into the station.

"Ask her when you see her again," he said. I got onto the train. I could still feel him inside me, and when I thought about what we had done, how it had felt when he was inside me, I felt the thrill that I'd felt the first time I looked at him.

It wasn't that different from what I'd felt with other men I'd been with, but it had been exciting to be with him. I thought about him later when I was at home. So I went back two weeks later, bored and looking for a new thrill, as teenagers will do.

We talked more this time. I didn't mention you, and neither did he. He let me read some of the things he was working on and showed me pictures of himself when he was a kid. Curious like you, he said. Always asking questions, looking for answers that aren't there.

That was the first week of September. School was starting two days later. I was more at ease then with him, conversation was easier. I smoked a cigarette. He drank half a beer.

We undressed in the living room. I don't think either of us really intended to have sex, but it just happened. I left my clothes in a pile on the floor near the couch like before. Sex was better this time, conversation came easily afterward, and I let slip that school was starting in a couple of days.

"So what college are you heading to?" he asked.

The look on my face must have told him I'd been lying. "You're not eighteen yet, are you? Oh, Christ, Rose! Why did you tell me that shit?"

He stood up, exasperated, shook his head, then got back into bed.

"Jesus Christ! Listen to me, girl, you can't tell anyone what we did here, and you can *never* come over here again. Never! Don't you know that I could do serious time in Rikers for what we've just done?"

"And I'm not worth going to jail for?" I joked with a pretty smile. That was when we heard the door open, when you called out his name.

"Stay here," he said. "Don't move."

Mariah

thirteen

$\mathcal{I}$ take over from where Rose has left off.

I stood outside his door for five minutes, then took my key and stepped into the hall. There was a short foyer that led into the living room, with a kitchen off that. Another short hall led to the bathroom and on the right was the bedroom. Not exactly a railroad apartment, but close to it. I stood in the foyer getting my bearings, then went into the living room. The windows were open, but the shades were pulled up and flapping slightly in the breeze. The light on his electric typewriter was on. The desk light was burning. A half-empty bottle of beer was on the desk next to the light. Something German. Löwenbräu Dark.

So he was here.

"Durrell." I called out his name, but not too loudly. I didn't want any trouble. I didn't want him to think I was still mad or being aggressive or nasty. I was going to be "nice," cooperative. We hadn't spoken since I left and I had finally begun to find peace within myself.

I had forgiven myself for falling in love with him. Distance had given me a sense of objectivity. I had made the biggest mistake of my life, no doubt about that, but neither of us was truly to blame for what had happened between us. It had just happened, like walking down the street and some crazy fool runs smack into you and knocks you down—not bad enough to kill you, but hard enough to knock the wind out of you for a while, hard enough to make you lose your breath.

But then you catch it again. You stand back up. Wipe the dirt off your clothes and keep getting up. It was just one of those things, like that song says. What happened between me and Durrell Alexander was just one of those crazy things. It was time for me to accept it for what it was.

I kept remembering his face the night I told him I had left my husband to live with him. He didn't think I was actually going to do it. His eyes showed sheer panic, that was what had been in them. Maybe he was in love with me, too, but it had been a flirtation more than anything else. There were probably half a dozen unhappily married women he'd been involved with during the years he'd been in the city. More than likely they fell into his life, enjoyed the splendor of his body for a couple of months, then dutifully returned to their boring husbands. The filmmaker Durrell Alexander had been some interesting "dish" to share with their girlfriends over a martini at lunch.

Not me. I had taken it all too seriously. I didn't know how to flirt. Didn't know bullshit from the real thing. What was that expression my mother used to say about not knowing shit from shinola? Both he and Hilton had been shit. I had yet to see shinola, whatever the hell that was. We had brought the worst out in each other, and the sooner we both moved on—as far away from each other as we could get—the better off both of us would be.

If there had ever been friendship between us, any beauty at all, it was ugliness now. Lots of things had turned it bad, but mostly it had been what happened that night with Elias, as drugged-out and drunk as we all had been. I never wanted to see that part of me again.

But there was no use in crying about that, either. I hadn't had a drink or done a drug since I'd left him. Not even wine at dinner with Trish or grass while we watched TV.

Over and done with. Through. Moving on up,

like on that TV show *The Jeffersons*. Like what Trish was always saying: Forget the past, look forward to the future. Don't let anything hold you back. Her optimism was rubbing off on me.

I didn't think about Elias Belle.

For the first time in my life, I felt sure of myself. Trish had helped me find a job as a receptionist at the women's magazine where she worked, and it was empowering to be in the presence of independent, professional black women. It made me feel independent and professional, too.

I can do this! I'm a winner! Look out, world, here I come!

I must have whispered those affirmations a million times, so often that I finally believed them. I had glimpsed the possibility of living my life for myself, with nobody to answer to but myself and my kids. Trish had talked me into going back to school. I had a good business sense, she said, and with some of the government funding that was becoming available for women owning small businesses, I might even start my own. I was young, gifted, and black—to quote Lorraine Hansberry—and I had everything going for me.

I'd also talked to that lawyer, Lisa Bonavera, about getting back you and Dani. She had been outraged by the gall of your father, and assured me there was no way in hell a court would award sole custody to a father with young daughters.

Hilton was a bully and a thief, as far as she was concerned, and there was nothing she liked better than fighting bullies and thieves. She was actually looking forward to going up against him in court, she said. She had me looking forward to it, too.

So on that Saturday afternoon, I was sure I could handle anything that Durrell threw my way. It was Labor Day weekend, and like New Year's Eve or the first day of spring, it was a new beginning.

I hadn't left that much stuff at his place. I hadn't left home with that much. There were a few sweaters I'd need for fall, a few pieces of clothing I'd bought after I moved in, and some jewelry, a couple pairs of earrings. Mainly, I just wanted a clean break from him. A new page in the book of my life.

I stood for a while waiting for him to answer, then glanced down the hall toward the bedroom. The door was closed. But then I felt his presence; it passed through me like a chill. Maybe he was taking a nap. He did that when he'd been out late the night before. I used to tease him about it, the way he took naps in the middle of the day, like a kid or an old man. I wasn't sure yet which one he actually was: a mischievous boy or an evil old presence.

Maybe he was with somebody. I didn't like the feeling that came over me when I thought about that, and I shoved it out of my mind as fast as I could.

Hell, I didn't give a damn one way or the other, I told myself. Whoever she (or he was, if Trish was right about him), she or he could damn well have him. Good riddance! Take him out of my life for good. Just don't get high with him and another dude on a hot Friday night.

The thought of that night made me shiver, brought back the shame I'd felt then, with their grabbing, stroking hands all over my body. It made me want to run out of that room, right into the street. Then I could come back another day. Call him first. Forget about the damn things altogether.

I toyed with how that conversation would go:

"I want my things, Durrell," I'd say to him on the phone. "Put them out in the hall. I'll pick them up when I can."

"Come and get them!" he'd say back in that taunting drawl that made me want him even when I told myself I didn't. "Just come over here and get them from me."

"Okay, I'm here," I said, now standing in the hall. But my voice was shaking.

"Durrell," I said it louder this time.

"Durrell. If you're here, I want my stuff. It's Mariah." *Maria.*

He was in the bedroom. I heard voices, his

mostly. I couldn't hear the other. I walked toward the door.

"Yeah, I'm here." He came out quickly, opened the bedroom door, slammed it closed behind him before I could get any closer. "Don't go in there."

He had slipped on his cutoff jeans, and they rode so low on his slender waist I could see a smattering of pubic hair. No shoes, no shirt. He smelled like sex. I knew there was a woman there, lying in his bed like I used to do, wanting him again like I always had.

I took a couple of steps back into the living room.

"I want my things," I said.

"No problem." We stood there staring at each other until he said, "What took you so long?" He walked to his desk. Turned off the typewriter, took a sip of beer, then went into the kitchen and poured it down the sink. I followed him.

"I packed all your shit up. It's in the bedroom. Don't go in there. I'll get it," he said.

"Don't worry, I'm not going into your damn bedroom. I don't want to run into whatever bitch you're fucking. Didn't take you long, did it? Or were you fucking her all the time?"

I was ashamed and angry. Ashamed because I knew how completely I had been taken in by him; angry because I had allowed myself to be used and lost everything that meant anything to me.

And because I still felt something. I don't know which feeling was stronger.

"Don't tell me you're jealous, Mariah."

"Maria."

"Back to that? Why am I not surprised? Well, what did you expect? What did you think was going to come of it?" He was suddenly the philosophical one, with his condescending, smartass nod.

"Just get my goddamn things," I said. "And whoever that stupid bitch is in your room, whoever it is you're fucking, I hope she knows what she's getting into."

I couldn't interpret the look he gave me, it was quick, amused, with a shadow of something else as well that I realized later must have been pity. I turned away from him, and he went back into the bedroom, said something to whomever it was, slammed the door again.

It was going on five, and the room was getting cool. The breeze coming in through the window was stronger. I glanced outside the window, wasting time, wondering again how I had let myself get so deeply into this thing with him. But it was over now, I reminded myself. Finally done. I would never have to see him again, never have to think about him.

Obsessive love. A writer had done a piece on that

subject for the magazine, and Trish had brought it home for me to read. I realized that I'd been *obsessed* with Durrell the year before I left, addicted to him. He'd been the morning drink a drunk needs to start her day, the shot of heroin that will land a woman on the street. One more month of him, and I would have ended up there, too. I glanced down the hall. Poor dumb bitch. At least it wasn't me.

I started to get nervous. What the hell was taking him so long? He said he'd packed my things up. He'd probably been lying. I hated the thought of some woman watching him pack my stuff—the jilted woman's belongings—I've got him now! she would think with a grin.

At least I'd taken the pictures of you and Dani with me, I thought. I wouldn't want any of his women touching those.

I glanced around the living room in disgust. He always left his junk lying around. Old newspapers, soiled clothes, half-finished bottles of wine and beer. I was used to seeing that. I noticed the clothing near the couch when I came in. Just some more of Durrell's junk, I figured. I used to pick up after him like he was a kid when I first moved in with him, like a maid or his damned mother.

Then something on this particular pile of junk caught my eye. Pink panties. Silk ones, edged with fancy lace. The delicate kind you don't dare wash with Tide or Cheer but with Dove, maybe Camay soap. Something tugged at my heart. Then I saw what lay beside them. A white linen blouse. The one I'd bought you last summer. Stylish and pretty. Didn't have to wear it with a bra, you said. Do you remember how we argued about that blouse because I said it was too grown-up, but I let you have it anyway because it made you look so pretty. Blue jeans. Thin-legged, tight. Brown leather belt looped on the jeans, the one that disappeared from my closet months before I left.

I didn't want to see. I didn't want to know.

It wasn't a scream that came out of me, but something else from so deep inside me it hurt when it left me. He met me halfway down the hall.

"Don't go in there!" He was dragging a black plastic bag behind him like some demented Santa Claus. He put it down. Pushed me back into the living room. I started hitting him as hard as I could on his face, on his chest, anywhere my hands could reach. I didn't want to see, smell, or think about what had happened between you.

There were no words ugly enough to call him. No words could tell the hatred that I felt. No words had been invented. All I could do was scream your name. "Rosie!"

He slapped me hard. I scratched him across his face, aiming at his eyes, scratched at his eyelids, then at his mouth and across the nose. I felt his flesh underneath my nails. He screamed and hit me, and I fell on the floor.

I didn't recognize my voice when I said your name again. "Rosie!"

"This isn't your business," he said. I pulled away from him, heading toward the bedroom. He snatched me away, and I bit his hand as hard as I could, drawing blood. I could taste it salty on my tongue. I spit it out.

"What the fuck is wrong with you!" he said.

I couldn't think. There were no words in my mind. All I could do was spit and scratch and scream. He wiped my spit from his face, drawing back, and slapped me hard again. I fell on the floor and kicked him in the groin, he yelled out, and I got up, headed toward the room to reach you. He grabbed my arm, pulled me back, and I fell backward onto the floor. I pulled myself up, supporting myself on the edge of his old maple bureau. The lion-shaped handles scratched my hands.

Blood ran down his face from my scratches. We both panted hard, our eyes fixed on one another, cutting through flesh to our souls. I remembered the first time we'd made love, how much we had wanted each other, how the sound of his breath made me want him inside me more, and I wanted to be sick, vomit up every piece of him that had ever been there.

Suddenly you stood in the doorway, bare-breasted and frightened, your thin little body uncovered except for his t-shirt tied loosely around your waist. I ached with love for you.

"Stop it," you said. "Please stop it!"

"Why?" was the only word I could say. He answered for you.

"Because she wanted it as much as you did," he told me.

I can't remember opening the drawer where I knew he kept the gun, but of course I must have done it—opened it, pulled out the gun, aimed it. I remember the cold hardness of it in my hand, but I don't know if I felt it before or after I pulled the trigger.

There was nothing in his eyes when he fell, not anger or even surprise, just a glance like you might give some stranger who catches your eye on the subway. Indifferent, as if there had never been anything between us at all.

Your screams were what brought me back.

We held each other that day, do you remember that, Rosie? How tightly we held each other, your small naked breasts against my own. I felt your sobs inside me.

"You can't tell anyone you were here," I told you. "Do you understand?"

You couldn't see or hear me. I slapped your face

hard, like you just did mine. "Do you understand?"

You nodded that you did. I dressed you like I did when you were a little girl, each piece placed on your trembling body until you stood before me as you had come to him.

"Promise me that whatever happens, you won't tell!" I told you.

You wouldn't look at me.

"Answer me, Rosie. Promise!"

We had only a moment before someone called the cops. Only a moment.

I got the money he kept in the bureau beside the gun. I looked outside the apartment. Nobody was there. I was lucky that day. I took you downstairs. We walked a few blocks, and I put you in a cab, and told the driver to take you back to Jersey and keep the change. Then I went upstairs and called the cops myself.

After I finish, my daughters are silent. The window is open, and from somewhere outside I hear a child laugh so sweetly and clearly it brings tears to my eyes. I look at my girls, Rose and Dani, both women now, sitting close to me like they did when I would tell them stories. But this had been the truth.

Sunday

Dani

fourteen

*I*t is well after midnight. Rose glances at her watch and hints that it is time for us to leave. We hug our mother goodbye, and she gives us her phone number and asks if we will call her later. I tell her I will; Rose says nothing.

On the way home, I think about my father's words to me on the morning he died, him telling me to open that door like he did, and how it hadn't made any sense. How much of what they told me tonight did he know?

"Did you ever tell Daddy what happened?"

"Daddy? When was the last time you called him that?"

"It just came out." It surprises me as much as it does her.

"No, this was the first time I've talked to anybody about it. Tonight with you and her."

"Well, that damned door he was talking about is finally open," I say, and Rose gives me her classic sideways glance, lips slightly parted, eyebrows raised half an inch, then looks back at the road.

"The thing about doors, Dani, is that once they're open, you never know what's going to walk through them, and it's hard to close them again. I'm sure Pop knew that."

"Like he did everything else?"

"Not everything."

I wonder if he had been telling me to let Mariah back into my life, if somehow he knew she would show up when he died, and this was his last blessing.

"Well, it's open now, and Mariah is back."

"Maria."

"Mariah," I said. "I like it better than Maria. It suits her."

"That was what *he* called her."

"I don't care what *he* called her. She's my mother, and I can call her whatever the hell I want," I say, then, realizing I sound like that petulant child Rose sees so often, soften my voice. "What about you? What will you call her?"

Rose turns on the radio without answering. Ever since I've been a kid that has been her sign that she doesn't want to talk. I turn it down, my sign that I am determined to.

"So how do you feel about her now?" I push her.

Her eyes dart back to me. "For a long time, I felt nothing but anger, but I don't even feel that anymore. I pity her now." Then she adds, almost to herself as an afterthought, "Some things are unforgivable."

"Like what, Rose? That she left us to run off with her lover or that she loved you enough to kill him?" I was ready to run off with Ben, after all. I hadn't thought about Teddy, not like I should have, anyway. How could I hold her responsible when I had felt those feelings, too?

"It's not so much her as myself, Dani," she says. "That I started the relationship with Durrell in the first place, for spite more than anything else, that I'm the reason a man is dead, and that she made me keep it to myself."

"She did it to protect you."

Rose sighs. "Yeah, I guess she did. But it changed something inside me, too. It made me into somebody I wasn't."

"You didn't have to keep it to yourself. You could have come home and told Aunt Lu what happened."

"But I couldn't without betraying her."

"That's not her fault!"

"It's no one's fault. But that doesn't change the way I feel. When things cause too much pain, you have to cut them out because it hurts too much to hold onto them, and I tore her out of me that night. There's nothing left of her inside me to take root."

I'd ripped out Mariah, too, but there was still enough of her inside me to grow again.

"I'm glad to finally know the whole story." I pull out the brooch I had pinned to my slip earlier that day and show it to Rose. "I should have given her this tonight. I forgot I had it."

"You've kept it all these years?"

I pin it on my suit this time, not inside. "I'll give it back to her next time I see her."

"Next time?"

"I told her I'd bring Teddy to meet her. Will you come with me?"

I'm not surprised when she doesn't answer.

"How long do you think it will take you to forgive her?"

"As long as it takes," she says, and I leave it at that.

Chance is waiting for me when I come home; all the lights are out.

"Dani—"

"Let's not talk now." He tries to embrace me,

and I pull away and sit on the opposite end of the couch.

We sit for a long time in the dark room in silence until I go upstairs and fall asleep on top of the bed. It is early when I awake, and Chance is sitting next to me, his hand resting gently on my back watching me like some guardian angel. I forget for a moment what had happened on Saturday. I just want to feel his arms around me, to feel safe like I do when he holds me.

"You know how much I love you," he says.

I nod because I do, but I have to let myself feel it again, inside my heart.

"I told Aunt Lu I'd bring Teddy over there and stay with her for a while." He lets his breath out slowly, which makes me think of Ben. "Aunt Lu needs the company, and it will give us time to decide what to do."

So later that day, Chance and I pack some of Teddy's things, and together we explain that Aunt Lu misses my father, and, generous child that he is, he is happy to keep her company. We will tell him the truth later, if it comes to that.

I don't kiss Chance good-bye when he leaves, but I tell him we can talk some more in the morning, after he takes Teddy to school. He whispers that he loves me, and I tell him I love him, too. But I don't know if that will be enough.

After I put Teddy to bed that night, him in my lavender-and-white bedroom, me in Rose's old bed, I think about Ben and how much I loved him. I know that his roots are still inside me but that he'd ripped mine out, the way Rose has done to our mother's because it cost him too much to keep them. And that makes me think again about Mariah and what Rose said about cutting her out of her heart. Will I have to cut Chance out of mine, I wonder, and if I do, how long will it take me to let him back in? As long as it takes, I decide.

Rose

fifteen

I need to go to some-
place where I can slip out of myself, put everything I'm feeling in perspective, so I go to the
place where I'm most myself, where I meet Marshall on Fridays, "our room," with its long, narrow windows that look out on nothing, and its
bed so comfortable with memories.

When I get there, I shower, down half a glass of
merlot, and fall asleep reading one of the novels I
keep there. In the morning, I call Marshall and
leave a message on his cell, asking if he can come
to our room as soon as he can. I go out and buy
Italian pastries, Costa Rican coffee for me, the
spicy ginger tea he loves, and a bunch of roses.
Red ones. I'm not sure why. When Marshall
comes, we sit on the bed and I tell him what I told
Dani last night, about what happened between

Durrell Alexander, my mother, and me. When I finish, he sips his tea and is silent for so long it scares me.

"That bastard got what he deserved," he finally says. They are harsh words for my Marshall, and I know he is thinking about his daughter and what he would do if that had happened to her.

"He paid with his life. Does that really seem a fair price to you?"

"Maybe not," he admits after a moment. "But what about her, your mother? She paid with her life, too. And so did you, for his lack of control."

"I don't know much about his life, but I suspect there were reasons for his 'lack of control,' as you put it, that put him in the position he found himself in. He thought I was eighteen. That was what I told him."

"But he knew you were his lover's daughter. Don't make excuses for the son of a bitch."

"He's dead, Marshall," I say gently. "He was younger than I am now, and he's dead."

He sighs, nods, gives me that. "So when will you see her again? Maria?"

"I've lived too long without her in my life," I say, but that is a quick, easy answer. The real one is more complicated. I had seen my mother shoot to death a man with whom I had just made love. The stillness in his dead face and the hatred I saw in hers will be with me forever.

He interprets my silence correctly. "So you're going to let her go."

Maria Dells is a sad, wounded woman and my heart always softens for sad, wounded people, but it is like I told Dani, I feel nothing but pity, and pity isn't a basis for the kind of relationship she yearns to have with me. I would always be lying to her, and I have told enough lies for one lifetime.

"Forgiving and forgetting is not just a matter of saying I forgive and forget," I say.

"No, but that's usually the first step, believing you can say it."

"I'm not ready to take that step yet."

"Maybe someday you will be. You have a big heart, Rose, capable of more love than you imagine."

"I hope so," I say, because maybe he is right. "Thank you for coming over here like you did." I change the subject, tired of talking about my mother. I reach for another pastry and notice the quick, furtive glance he gives his watch.

"Time for you to go?" I am thankful that I've gotten even this.

"You deserve more, and so do I."

I give him a bite of my pastry and think about how brides feed their grooms on their wedding day, which makes me smile. A piece of cream falls on his chin and I kiss it off.

"Friday then?"

He drops his eyes, and my heart stops. I know he sees the fear in them. "We need to talk about what we are going to do from now on. I won't go on like this, Rose. I can't lie to my family anymore. It's killing an essential part of me that I've always been proud of, my sense of integrity. I won't allow that to happen anymore. I've let it go on far too long, and I've grown ashamed of it. Do you understand that?"

"I'm tired of lying, too," I say, and as he stands to go, I grab his hand and pull him back down beside me. "I need to tell you something else."

I tell him about the lump in my breast and how frightened I am, and about not returning the doctor's calls. I tell him how I get sick to my stomach every morning when I feel it in the shower.

"Show it to me," he says.

"I don't want to."

He gently takes off my blouse and unhooks my bra. I close my eyes and guide his fingers to where it is, and when I open them, his eyes are filled with tears. He touches it carefully, as if his fingers can heal it, then kisses the space around it.

I understand then that his touch will heal me, too.

Mariah

sixteen

*S*he was the last person in this world I expected to see. I wouldn't have been more surprised if her brother himself, shaking dirt from his shroud, had shown up glowering and fussing at my door.

"May I come in?" Her manner was as stiff and formal as always. I paused before I let her pass, staring at her as if she were one of my ghosts. "I'm Lucille Dells, Hilton's sister."

"I know who you are." I stepped out of her way, and she walked into my living room proper as can be, looking neither to the left nor to the right, then sat down on my couch.

But no one, not even Lucille Dells, could dampen my mood this day. I'd gotten very little sleep; sheer happiness had kept me from it. The elation of being near them again, touching their faces, hearing voices I'd only heard in my dreams, had kept me awake. After they left, I'd dropped to my knees and prayed, thanking God for his mercy, for bringing my daughters back to me again.

Nothing Rose told me about her relationship with Durrell had surprised me. I knew too well the traps he could set, how easily one could stumble into them. Elias Belle had taught me that, but some things are too shameful to share.

So I had nothing to fear from Lucille Dells on this Sunday morning. I was more curious than anything else when I sat across from her. I wondered why she had come, what she could say to me after all those years.

She had always been an elegant dresser, with the style, I suspected, Hilton wanted for me. Her gray silk suit was well tailored, and the pearls around her neck were the real thing. She looked out of place in my drab little room, and I was embarrassed for a moment at the state of it but determined not to show it; I still had that much pride.

"Do you mind if I smoke?" she asked, and I searched for the ashtray I kept in a drawer, left long ago by some previous tenant.

"Could I get you something to drink? Tea, coffee? It's early in the day, but I have some gin or vodka if you'd like something stronger." Was I being too accommodating, too polite to this woman who had treated me so cruelly?

"If you have some orange juice, it's not too early for a screwdriver, if you'll have one with me," she said, then smiled with a surprising glimmer of good humor. She had always had a nice smile; I remembered that. But it was a smile that could turn nasty or sarcastic with the slightest turn of her lips. However, there was an edge of gentleness now that hadn't been there before. Had raising my girls changed her so much?

"Dani gave me your address when we spoke last night. She called me from here." She lit her cigarette with an elegant gold lighter that matched the gold cigarette case. I noticed the diamond ring on her finger, Hilton's mother's ring that had once belonged to me.

"Rose gave it to me several days ago," she said, her gaze following mine. "Hilton gave it to her shortly after you left, but she was never comfortable wearing it."

"Then it's back where it belongs," I said as I headed to the kitchen to make our drinks. I had taken out a can of orange juice to thaw for my breakfast tomorrow. I mixed it with water and then some vodka and poured it over ice.

"We've come full circle, Mariah," she said when I brought them back to the living room. She tapped mine lightly as if it were a toast. "Our girls are grown women, and we're too old to hold a grudge."

"I never held one."

"I did."

"And my name is Maria."

"Mariah who calls herself Maria," she said with a slight, wry smile.

"I guess you could put it that way."

A shadow came into her eyes. "I'm sorry."

"For what?"

"For what's happened to you."

I was offended but tried hard not to show it. Who the hell did she think she was, feeling sorry for me?

"I made my choices, and I've lived with them. And my life is not over yet," I said, holding my head unnaturally high.

Neither of us spoke after that but sipped our drinks, avoiding one another's eyes.

"Do you think you'll stay here? In this town?" She broke our tense silence.

Was that why she had come? To find a way to ask me to go? She was a powerful woman, and if she decided to use that power to force me out of town there wasn't a damn thing I could do.

"Yes. I'm here to stay. My girls are here. And my grandson. Our grandson." I gave her that, she deserved it. "I heard him call you 'Grandma' yesterday at the memorial."

"That's who I am to him."

"Is that why you came to see me this morning, to find out if I was going to live here?"

"No. I wanted to see who you had become."

"And who do you think I've become?"

"I'm not sure yet. Except that I know you mean Rose and Dani no harm."

"And do you really think I could harm my own children?"

"You did once," she said.

I was so angry I wasn't sure if I could contain it. To keep from saying or doing something I would regret, I picked up our drinks and headed back into the kitchen, bent over the sink, felt its hard coldness against my stomach, and counted to ten. My years in Somerset had taught me always to conceal strong feelings, never to show what I felt.

She followed me into my kitchen, and I felt hot, the room suddenly grown small and tight. I wanted to run out of the apartment, yell at her to leave, but I did nothing, then hated myself for not having the will to throw her out. Then she spoke.

"I don't know you, Maria, but I think I would like to now."

"Why?" I backed away from her, not sure of myself or of her.

"Because they belong to both of us," she said. "Dani and Rose are yours as much as mine. I can't expect you to stop loving them any more than you can expect that of me."

We went back into the living room, the tension now gone. I sat in the chair across from her, not sure what to say next. She lit another cigarette, exhaling elegantly, but her hand trembled, and I realized that she was as wary of me as I was of her. She was also uncomfortable and frightened; loving my daughters had made her vulnerable, too.

"Do you think you will see them again?" she asked.

"Dani said she would bring the boy over." Simply saying those words made me smile.

"Good. Dani needs you in her life. She's going through a terrible time, and she'll need all the support she can get. From both of us. And Rose?"

"I don't think Rosie will see me again." Until I said it to Lucille, I hadn't really admitted it to myself, and the acknowledgment brought tears to my eyes. Had it been jealousy that made me pull that trigger? I hadn't been able to answer Rose's question last night. I wasn't sure if I ever would be able to answer it. I didn't know myself.

"Rose is stubborn like her father, but she has a forgiving nature. Give her time," she said, then did something that surprised me. She reached across the table and took my hand in hers. Her touch was strong and confident, and I knew that my girls had felt these hands on them and been made strong because of them. "Give her time, Maria. She's Hilton's daughter, but there's a lot of me in her, too. And of you."

She told me that I could call her if I needed anything, money, advice or just to talk, and I told her that I would—for the sake of my girls—our girls—as much as for myself.

"Thank you for taking care of my daughters, for helping them get through what I did to them, for being the mother I couldn't be," I told her as she was leaving. They were hard words to say, but they had to be said. I knew it as well as she did. She smiled, nodded, then left.

My shift starts early tomorrow. I have to catch a bus at 5:00 A.M. to get there by the time the store opens. As I iron my uniform for work, I think about Irish and realize how much I'm looking forward to seeing her tomorrow morning. Maybe I will share what has happened to me over these three days.

"Maria! This is so exciting! Why didn't you tell me any of this before," she will say, and the thought of her funny lilting voice makes me smile. Maybe it is time I tell her just how much of a daughter she has become. My heart is becoming big enough now for anyone who wants to enter.

I turn on the oven to bake the chicken legs I'd taken from the freezer earlier, put water on for rice, pour myself the second of my evening drinks, then settle back on my couch. The day is ending, and I am happy. I know it will take years to make right what I did to my daughters, but we have talked, taken that first step, and my heart is no longer breaking.

Light from the street softens the shadows in my room. I close my eyes and listen to the sound of laughter outside, to music drifting in from down the hall. From somewhere, Mahalia Jackson is singing "Come Sunday." I sing along, my tuneless voice blending with her splendid one. Trish once told me Duke Ellington had written that song. There were so many things Trish tried to teach me, it's just taken me a while to learn them. Suddenly, I feel her spirit, and I know that she is with me.

"Shining times will find you, too," she'd said the day I left Durrell Alexander. Trish believed I could be happy even when I was sure I never could. I know now that happiness is possible for me, too.

I raise my glass in salute to my dear old friend. Maybe those shining times she promised me are finally on their way.

Soulful Love With A New Attitude

Sexy/Dangerous
by Beverly Jenkins
0-06-081899-7/$6.99 US/9.99 Can.

Schooling Carmen
by Kathleen Cross
0-06-114390-1/$6.99 US/9.99 Can.

Brickhouse
by Rita Ewing
0-06-113999-8/$6.99 US/9.99 Can.

Get Some Love
by Nina Foxx
0-06-113997-1/$6.99 US/9.99 Can.

Diary of an Ugly Duckling
by Karyn Langhorne
0-06-084755-7/$6.99 US/9.99 Can.

Hidden Sins
by Selena Montgomery
0-06-079849-1/$6.99 US/9.99 Can.

A Taste of Reality
by Kimberla Lawson Roby
0-06-082548-0/$6.99 US/9.99 Can.

Black Lace
by Beverly Jenkins
0-06-081593-0/$6.99 US/9.99 Can.